INVITATION TO DIE

Giff Ballew and Tucker Weybright traveled the road in silence. Giff reined up and turned in his saddle for a last look at his boyhood home.

Tucker's voice interrupted his thoughts. "Take a good look at it, you joker, because you'll never see it again. If you try, I'll draw you to our line with a rope."

"Sure, you're tough," Giff said drily. "There's nobody better when it comes to shooting drunks." He saw a wild temper flare in Tucker's eyes and he jibed, "Go ahead and shoot. I haven't got a gun."

Tucker reined in. He was white around the mouth. He pulled Giff's gun from his own waistband and tossed it to the ground ahead of Giff's horse.

"You got one now."

LUKE SHORT

FIRST CLAIM

A DELL BOOK

Published by
Dell Publishing
a division of
Bantam Doubleday Dell Publishing Group, Inc.
666 Fifth Avenue
New York, New York 10103

ISBN: 0-440-20455-0

Reprinted by arrangement with the author's estate

Printed in the United States of America

Published simultaneously in Canada

September 1989

10 9 8 7 6 5 4 3 2 1

KRI

First Claim

Chapter One

THE HOSTLER, standing in the runway of Harmony's only livery stable, saw almost simultaneously two happenings that interested him this windy May morning.

Old man Weybright, straight as a pine and almost as tall, left the opposite boardwalk and cut heedlessly into the heavy mid-morning traffic of teams and wagons. He was on a collision course with a laboring team but he did not alter that course a foot. The teamster called to him, but instead of heeding, Weybright simply slugged the nearest lead horse in the nose. The horse yanked it's head up, halted, and Weybright kept on. Ahead was another team going in the opposite direction. Weybright grabbed the cheek strap of the lead horse and turned it so that he did not have to vary his direction. Both drivers were cursing him now but Weybright did not so much as bother to look at them. He achieved the sidewalk and went on.

The second happening that interested the hostler was a rider approaching the livery. He was on the wrong side of the street, breasting traffic so that it had to pull out for him. He seemed to be studying the names on the stores and on the office windows above them. He too was tall, dressed in rough range clothes and dust-colored Stetson, and he was equally heedless of the teamsters' cursing. If the hostler had been a philosopher he would have remarked to himself that these must be two stubborn men. He was to remark it later.

The strange rider on a bay with a strange brand reined in by the hostler, dismounted and handed over his reins. "Grain him," he said in a pleasant voice. Then he added, "A lawyer name of Parry has his office on this street, doesn't he?"

His was a weather-scoured face, long-jawed and not recently shaven. His blue eyes were tranquil under thick jutting black brows and a pleasant humor seemed to light them just beneath their surface. His vest was buttonless and he wore a yellow cavalry neckerchief whose folds were gray with dust. He could have been thirty, no more.

The hostler gestured with his thumb. "He moved around the corner. Two doors down and upstairs."

The rider nodded. "Store that stuff in your office and I'll pick it up later," he said, nodding toward his blanket roll and carbine. Then he turned and headed down-street, his gait stiff-legged enough that the hostler guessed he had been some days in the saddle.

Achieving the head of the stairs of the second building around the corner and turning around the banister the rider saw painted on the first door to his right the legend SETH PARRY, ATTORNEY and palmed open the door. He was in a small room which was a combination waiting room and law library. Through an open door he saw an even smaller room with windows on the street. It contained a roll-top desk at which was seated a gray-haired man, his back to him.

At the sound of the closing door, the man rose and came into the reception room. He was slight, dressed in townsman's black and his aging face held a controlled reserve.

"Mr. Parry?" the rider asked.

The older man dipped his head in acknowledgment and now the rider said, "I'm Giff Ballew, Tom Ballew's son. Remember him?"

"I should say I do," Parry said warmly and extended his hand. "I remember you, too, as a shaver." He gestured toward his office. "Come in and sit down, won't you?"

Parry proceded Ballew into the office, gestured toward a stright-back armchair and seated himself in the swivel chair before his desk.

"Well, tell me about yourself," Parry said. "How's your father?"

"I'm sorry to have to tell you he died about three weeks ago."

"I'm sorry to hear that." His tone of voice seemed genuine to Ballew.

"Before he died he asked me to be sure and look you up when I came to Harmony." Ballew paused. "He said you'd been his good friend when the trouble happened."

Parry nodded. "I heard from Tom a couple of times and then lost track of him."

"He finally wound up in Wyoming. We have a fair-sized ranch that I ran until Dad died. My sister and her husband have it now."

"You're on the loose then?" Parry asked.

"Not at all," Ballew said. "I've come to claim our place."

Parry looked puzzled.

"The place the government seized from us in sixty-two under the Civil War Confiscation Act of eighteen sixty-two."

"But that was seventeen years ago," Parry said. "It was a legal seizure, since your father was accused and convicted of bearing arms against the Union, and the place was auctioned off."

Ballew said slowly, "I don't know much law, Mr. Parry, but I do know my father said that President

Lincoln softened that law. Wasn't it rewritten to read that a rebel's lands and goods were seized and auctioned, but the lands were to revert to his heirs upon his death?"

Parry nodded, frowning. "That's true. But I've never heard of a case involving reversion to heirs coming before the law here."

"Here's one," Ballew said quietly. "I'm an heir to the estate of Tom Ballew. His lands that were auctioned off rightfully belong to me."

Parry frowned and picked up a ruler from his desk and gently tapped his fingers with it, staring at the wall behind Giff's head. "Your father had a deed to these lands?" he asked.

"He had one, but it was lost during the war," Ballew said. "Dad bought the ranch from Herbert Ellice who had it on a patent from the government. Surely the records will show the transfer from Ellice to Ballew."

"Possibly," Parry said unenthusiastically. He looked down at his hand and gently slapped the palm of it with the ruler. "I wonder if you realize what you're undertaking." He looked directly at Giff now. "People on that land have had it for seventeen years. They've improved it and built on it. They'll not willingly leave. If it comes to a contest at law no jury would be willing to vote them off. That's just human nature."

Giff said quietly, "I look at it another way. They've had free use of that land for seventeen years. The intention of Lincoln's act was to punish the men who bore arms against the Union and not to punish their children." He grinned wryly. "I think the Ballews have been punished enough. Especially since my father's conviction was gotten on perjured evidence."

"That I believe, and I said so at the time," Parry said.

"Then will you act as my lawyer and handle this case?"

Now Parry tossed the ruler onto the desk and looked at Giff. "Son, I would like to for the sake of my friendship with your father, but I simply can't do it."

"Why not?"

"I know the man who bought your father's property at government sale. I have been attorney on his behalf

for more than ten years. My first obligation is to him."
He added, "I'm really sorry."

Giff felt his face flush and he knew that he had made
a serious mistake. Had Parry pumped him intentionally?
Certainly Parry now had all the facts and a rough idea
of Giff's plans. He rose. "Then you'll likely be attorney
for—Weybright. Isn't that the name?"

Parry nodded. "Very likely—if the court decided to
hear it."

"Why wouldn't it?"

Parry smiled thinly. "I don't propose to tell you as
much as you told me, son. Can't we leave it at that?"
He rose too, and held out his hand. "I'm sorry I can't
do a favor for the son of an old friend. On anything
else I'd be more than glad to help."

Giff accepted his hand and Parry showed him to the
door. Tramping down the stairs, Giff cursed himself.
He had accepted his father's evaluation of Seth Parry,
forgetting that men change because they have to change.
Doubtless Weybright was a prosperous man with much
legal work. Long ago Parry had protested the conviction *in absentia* of Tom Ballew who, faced with lying
witnesses, had fled the country; but Parry also had a
living to make among these people he had chosen to
live with. Weybright's money was as good as anyone's.

Once on the street Giff looked about him. On his ride
here he had had the notion that he would look up the
men who had refused to give testimony against his
father. Then it had been his idea to talk with them and
to thank them for past favors. Now, in view of what
Parry had said, he might need them for something else.
If he must prove that his father had bought his land
from Ellice, then these men could help. He knew some
of their names but he did not know if they had moved
out of the country, or even if they were still alive. The
newspaper office with its files could give him the full
list.

Accordingly, he asked the first passer-by where he
could find the newspaper office and was told it was a
block down on the same side of the street. As he tramped

down the boardwalk he looked about him, reaching back into memory to the time he was twelve years old, trying to remember the old town. The brick bank on the corner was unchanged, but many of the old adobe buildings so common to this part of New Mexico had been replaced by false-front frame stores, some of which were badly in need of paint. The town was bigger and the old courthouse which had been a frame building, only a series of rooms with the Masonic Hall above it, was gone. He guessed that the two-story brick building he could see up the street was probably the new courthouse.

In the next block he halted before a narrow one-story frame building whose wide windows were painted white to the height of a tall man. In black letters was painted the legend *SAN DIMAS COUNTY TIMES*. In smaller letters beneath it was painted PRINTING, STATIONERY AND REAL ESTATE.

He palmed open the door and stepped into one of the most magnificently cluttered rooms he had ever seen. Against the window was a big square table piled almost chest high with papers, proofs, books, and boxes. In a sort of well made by this clutter was a six-gun lying on a tablet, as if the editor was ready and willing to battle for what he printed. The most conspicuous object was a huge dictionary that measured a good nine inches in thickness. An old wardrobe with a sagging door was against the far partition and atop it were stacked dusty files of old newspapers. He could hear a press clattering beyond the partition, and when he closed the door its unoiled hinges cried out.

Almost immediately a girl stepped through the door in the partition. She was slight and wore a skirt and blouse of matching dark blue; her sleeves were protected almost up to the elbows by pinned cuffs of newsprint which was smudged. Giff took this in at a glance as he touched his hatbrim. This was a sober-faced girl, he thought immediately, with the palest hair he had ever seen piled carelessly atop her head. Her eyes were almost black and her full eyebrows shades darker than her hair. She could have been twenty-five he guessed, and, as she moved into the room, light caught the sparkle of her wedding ring.

"Are you after Sam?" she asked. "He's back in the shop."

"Is he the editor?"

The girl nodded.

"Maybe I won't have to bother him," Giff said. "I wonder if I could have a look at your files?"

"Oh, Lord. That takes in a lot of territory. This paper started in the middle fifties." She brushed a whisp of hair from her forehead. "What year are you after?"

"Sixty-three."

She crossed the room and opened the door to the wardrobe. It came off its hinges and fell toward her. Giff made a lunge to catch it. The door in its angling fall rapped the girl smartly on the head and before Giff could catch it he heard her explosive "Damn!"

Giff held the door and watched her rub her forehead in a grimace of pain.

"If I've done that once I've done it fifty times," she said bitterly. "Sam can repair a press, but he can't fix a hinge."

"Husbands are like that," Giff said.

"He's not my husband or this *would* be fixed," the girl said flatly. Then she smiled and the soberness fled from her face. "I'm Mrs. Miles. Sam's name is Furman. I think he neglects this door on purpose, just to ambush me."

"My name's Giff Ballew," Giff said. And he added, "You'll likely have a bump."

"I know, I know," Mrs. Miles said impatiently. "I always do."

Giff took the door and fitted it back on its hinge after pushing back a newspaper that had elevated the door off its hinge.

Inside he could see crudely bound files of the *Times,* the years marked on the back of the binding. He pulled out the volume that was inked 1863 close to the bottom of the pile and, turning, saw Mrs. Miles gesture toward the desk. "I don't think that weighs quite enough to cave in the legs. Want to put it there?"

Giff took the files over to the cluttered desk and opened the cover which was of heavy poster paper.

Mrs. Miles came up to him. "You know what you're after? Maybe I can help."

"An account of the trial of Tom Ballew. I guess you'd call it a trial," Giff said slowly. "He'd left the country but he was accused and convicted of bearing arms against the Union."

Mrs. Miles frowned. "Let me ask Sam." She went back into the shop and Giff idly began leafing through the dusty pages that were beginning to yellow and color. At her return Giff looked up and saw that a man had followed her.

Sam Furman appeared to be a man not yet thirty. He was of middle height, slight and he wore an ink-stained canvas apron. His hands were even more ink-stained and he had a harried expression on his thin face that bordered on impatience. His curly chestnut hair was awry, his voice abrupt as he said, "That Ballew hearing was in the month of March. Here, I'll find it for you."

"Ballew," Mrs. Miles said curiously. "Didn't you say your name was Ballew?"

"Tom Ballew was my father." To Sam he said, "How come you remember the month of the trial?"

"It was pretty famous in these parts. The old-timers still talk about it." He leafed over to the March issues and finding what he wanted tapped the paper. "There's the story."

Now Furman looked curiously at Giff. "The hearing ran five days as I recall it. The first week's issue of the paper carried the testimony of the man who swore your father had talked sedition and was in touch with the Texans who had marched for Santa Fe. The next week's issue had the testimony of character witnesses who denied the previous evidence."

"The second issue is the one I want," Giff said quietly.

"It's none of my business, but what for?" Furman asked.

"I want to see if any of these men are still around here."

Furman looked curiously at him and then turned to

the next issue; using his finger as a guide he went through the page-one story. "Inglehart is dead, Parry is here, Bohanan moved over east, Sydenham is dead, and Keefer is very much alive. That's Mrs. Miles's father."

Giff glanced at the girl. "Would your father talk to me?"

"I don't see why not. What about, though?"

Giff explained then that he had returned here on his father's death to claim the lands which would revert to Tom Ballew's heirs. He explained the lost deed and the need to establish legally that his father had owned the land of which he had been dispossessed and which was now occupied by the Weybright family.

"Lynch Weybright, you mean!" Sam said.

"That's right."

Giff surprised Mrs. Miles regarding him with dead soberness, so he said, "I hope your father will be willing to help me."

Mrs. Miles looked at him a long time and then shrugged. "You can always ask him," she said coldly. She turned and went back into the shop and now Giff, puzzled, looked at Sam. "What did I say?"

"Local politics," Sam said drily, then corrected himself, "No, not politics either. You're just opening old wounds."

Giff waited, frowning, for elaboration, and Furman seemed to hesitate.

Then Furman said, almost to himself, "No, I don't suppose you ever heard of what happened after your family left."

"Not a word."

Sam took a deep breath. "Your father owned considerable range. After he pulled out, a dozen outfits moved onto it. They knew it was illegal, and that an auction was coming. They got together and agreed not to bid against one another and to let one man bid for the whole parcel. He wouldn't bid much and they'd all chip in to pay for the land they'd squatted on."

"Sensible," Giff observed.

"It didn't turn out to be. The three Weybrights came

along, all outsiders. They outbid their man, hired a tough crew and threw all the outfits off. It was a rough and bloody time. Families called in their kin. Two Weybrights were killed and there was hardly a family in the dozen involved that didn't lose one or two men. Kate just doesn't want those times back."

"Was Keefer involved?"

"He was one of them."

That was why Mrs. Miles was reluctant to have him talk to her father: she didn't want him involved in Giff's legal quarrel with the Weybrights. Now Giff said, irony in his voice, "You make this Weybright sound pretty tall."

"He is. So's his sister and her husband, Todd Stoughton. They have adjoining ranches. Weybright has two sons and a crew that's never been curried. The two families pretty much run this county. If you quarrel with Circle W you've already quarreled with Bib S."

Giff smiled faintly. "I haven't."

"I'm not sure I would either," Sam said slowly. "Leave this to the courts. If your father once had a deed and recorded it, there's bound to be a record in the courthouse. Turn it over to the lawyers."

"Any here?"

"One. He's Weybright's."

"I found that out," Giff murmured.

Furman grinned. "Funny thing," he said reflectively, "when I came to Harmony it was partly because the name of the town attracted me. It suggested a lot of nice people getting along with one another." He added wryly, "Ha."

Giff thanked him and stepped out into the windy sunshine. Halting at the edge of the plankwalk he considered what Furman had told him. *Leave this to the courts,* he'd said. Maybe that was the wise thing to do, at that. Still, he'd like to know if there was any evidence a lawyer could go on, and he remembered Furman's suggestion to examine the courthouse records.

Now he turned toward the courthouse and within a half block the business part of town ended. Reaching the corner, he saw that the two-story brick courthouse with its cupola occupied a half block. Its unkept lawn held a couple of old cottonwoods. At the tie-rail in front of the door a half-dozen ponies stood with their rumps to the wind. As Giff approached the steps, he saw the lawn was littered with papers and bottles and cans. It occurred to him that these people couldn't be very proud of their government and its officials or of what they stood for if they tolerated this.

As he mounted the steps, the door swung open and a tall, white-haired man in range clothes came out. He was a handsome man and his lean face was bisected by dead-white mustaches. He looked sharply at Giff, nodded civilly and passed Giff, who nodded in return. Once in the courthouse corridor, Giff turned right. Each office was identified by a gilt-lettered sign over the door, and Giff tramped down to the back corner office which the sign proclaimed was the County Clerk and Recorder's domain.

Entering, he halted at a counter that barred his way. At his entrance a man who was seated at a slate-top desk got off his stool and came erect. He was a giant of a man with massive shoulders and great slabs of hands, and his townsman's shirt, trousers, and shoes seemed grotesquely inappropriate. Giff guessed that he was ranch-bred and that his presence here was by political chance.

The man came up to the counter and Giff nodded. "Are you the clerk?"

"Deputy clerk," the man said.

"Where can I find the clerk?"

"You can't. He's on vacation."

"Maybe you can help me," Giff said. "I want to check some of your records."

A caution came into the big man's face and he said, "Like what?"

"I want to see if a deed was recorded in the year eighteen sixty."

The big man said pleasantly, "I can't do it. That book would be in the vault and the vault is locked."

Giff hesitated, "Haven't you got a key?"

"The clerk took it with him," the big man said, a kind of insolence in his voice.

"Then how do you expect to do business while the clerk's away?"

"I'll make out all right."

Giff looked at him sharply. "When did the clerk start his vacation?"

The big man grinned. "Half an hour ago."

"And how long will he be gone?"

"He didn't say."

Giff knew then that the man was intentionally stalling. He said with an edge to his voice, "My friend, county records are public documents. Everybody has access to them."

The big man shrugged. "You got access to anything in this room."

"But not to the vault?"

"No."

Giff hesitated, "I think you're lying if you say you can't—"

The big man moved with a catlike quickness as he drove his fist into Giff's jaw. A second later from his position flat on the floor Giff dimly saw the big man hurdle the counter. Giff tried to struggle to his feet and suddenly found himself assisted by the big man yanking him erect. Through a swimming fog, Giff saw the second blow coming and was unable to do anything about it. The painful brightness before his eyes was suddenly drowned in blackness.

When he came to, he was lying face down in the corridor where the deputy had thrown him. The giant was lounging in the doorway of the clerk's office, filling it, his shoulder against the doorjamb. For a moment Giff bitterly regretted having stowed his gun and shell belt within his blanket roll. He was unarmed, dizzy, mad and helpless, and he knew it. Slowly he dragged himself to his feet as the world careened around him. He heard the big man say, "Never call a man a liar unless you can back it up, mister."

Giff turned and made his uncertain way out the door,

staggering from wall to wall. Once on the steps he shook his head again and drew in deep breaths of air. Slowly the world stopped spinning and then the anger returned.

Without a backward glance, Giff went down the steps, achieved the corner, and was soon abreast the newspaper office. He palmed open the door and saw the room was empty. Tramping to the desk, he reached across the clutter and picked up the six-gun. After checking the loads, he rammed it into his belt and sought the street again and tramped back to the courthouse.

In the corridor he lifted out his gun and walked slowly into the clerk's office. The big deputy was seated on the stool and, when he glanced up, Giff raised the gun.

Giff said thinly, "I can back it up now. You're a liar."

"You scare me," the big man said in a jeering voice.

Giff shot. The papers the deputy had been working on erupted like blown leaves. The deputy jumped off the stool, an expression of amazement in his face. "Why you damned fool—"

"The next one will be in your leg," Giff said. "Now open that vault."

The deputy stood irresolute, not speaking. The silence of the room was then interrupted by Giff cocking his gun.

"All right," the deputy said hastily. He took a key from a hook on the desk and moved over to the door of the vault. Now Giff swiftly opened the counter gate and came up behind him. There was the sound of running feet in the corridor and Giff eased the gun into the deputy's back before he rammed it in his belt. "You answer, my friend, and make it good," Giff said.

A voice called from the doorway then, "Who shot, Ed?"

The deputy called over his shoulder, "I just dropped my gun, Will, and it went off. No harm done." He swung the door open and stepped into the vault with Giff, gun now in hand, close behind him. The vault was a big one with a table inside. The deputy struck a match and lighted the table lamp, then skirted the table and began his search in a pile of big record books. He drew out one, put it on the table and then said, "What month?"

"July the fourteenth. Find me the record of the transfer of property from Herbert Ellice to Tom Ballew."

The deputy leafed through the book, then stopped. "Here's an entry June thirtieth." He moved his finger to the top of the following page. "This entry reads August second."

"Back off," Giff said curtly.

The deputy backed against the rear wall, and now Giff, gun in hand, bent over the book. The deputy was right as to his dates. Now Giff leaned closer and pressed on the book, spreading the pages. There, running from top to bottom of the book, was a thin sliver of paper against the binding. The page holding the record of his father's deed from Ellice had been neatly cut out; the last evidence of the transaction had been destroyed. *Leave this to the courts,* Furman had said. Leave what?

Giff rammed the gun in his waistband, looked at the deputy and said, "Come here." The big man pushed away from the wall, came over to Giff and halted before him. Without a word Giff slugged the man in the jaw. The deputy back-pedaled, tripped, and fell against the rear wall, rapping his head against the bricks. He sat there shaking his head.

"Surprised, eh? Well, so was I," Giff said. He turned and left the room and the building.

Kate Miles, needing a tablet to copy down the serial number for a part for the idle job press, first noticed that the gun had disappeared. Taking the tablet, she walked back into the shop, skirted the press and came up to Sam who was working at the stone.

"You packing a gun now?" she asked.

Sam looked up, puzzled. "No, why?"

"Your gun is gone from the desk."

Frowning, Sam tramped back into the office, Kate Miles trailing him. Halting at the desk, he stared at it and then pointed. "It was there a half hour ago." Now puzzled, he began to pull out and close the desk drawers.

He was still searching when the door opened and Giff Ballew entered. The big man tramped across the room, lifted a gun from his belt and extended it, butt first, to Sam. "I had to borrow this and I was kind of in a hurry."

Slowly Sam accepted the gun, then curiously held the end of the barrel up to the end of his nose and sniffed. He looked sharply at Giff. "You used it."

Ballew nodded and now Kate could not keep her surprise from showing in her face.

"No harm done," Giff said drily. "The deputy wasn't wanting to show me the deed book."

"So you shot him?" Sam said.

"Close to him."

"And what did the deed book show?" Sam asked.

"The page that held the recording had been cut out," Giff said tonelessly.

Kate looked at Sam and saw his mouth open in disbelief. "You mean the page has been destroyed?" Sam demanded.

Giff's broad shoulders lifted in a shrug and Kate could see a wicked anger in his pale eyes.

"Where does that leave you?" she asked.

"With no proof at all," Giff said grimly.

"Why, they can't do that!" Sam said hotly. "Who'd you talk with?"

"The deputy."

"Where was Larson, the clerk?"

"On vacation, the deputy said."

Giff went on to tell what had happened in the courthouse. When he was finished Sam looked briefly at Kate.

"This ought to rate a little write-up next week," Sam observed.

Kate only nodded, a dismal premonition of trouble coming to her.

"Can you tell me where I can find your father, Mrs. Miles?" Giff asked.

Kate answered almost with reluctance, "Our place is three miles south of town straight out this street."

Giff nodded and touched his hat, said, "Thanks for the loan," and stepped out, closing the door behind him.

Slowly now Sam placed the gun on the desk before glancing up at Kate. "What do you think of that story?"

"Watch out, Sam," Kate said quietly, "This is none of your affair."

"It's my affair if county records are destroyed!" Sam said angrily.

"You just have his word for it."

"You don't believe him?"

Kate shook her head. "It's not that, Sam. He's a troublemaker. You don't even know if he is what he says he is."

"Oh, come now, Katie girl." Sam's voice was dry, "What's got into you?"

Kate's lower lip quivered. "It's just that he'll rake up all those things that should be forgotten. If you side with him, you'll be in trouble. Right now he's on his way to get Dad into trouble." Angrily she wrenched off her paper cuffs. "Sam, I've got to get out there before he can talk with Dad." She bit her lip and said bitterly, "I wish I'd never seen the man. Why did he have to come here?"

"I imagine Weybright is asking himself the same question. The only difference is Weybright was ready for him."

"The missing page, you mean?"

"That's exactly what I mean," Sam said grimly, and now he yanked the strings of his apron. "Let's close shop, Kate. Run on home."

"While you do what?"

"I'm going over to the courthouse and see if Weybright was there today."

"It's bad enough that Ballew is stirring things up without you waiting for a turn at the stick," Kate said crossly.

"If a page can disappear out of a deed book then nobody's property in this county is safe." Sam's voice was righteous and angry.

He lifted the apron halter over his head, threw the apron on the desk and moved over to the wall where his coat and hat were hanging on a nail.

"Beat it, Katie. I'll see you in the morning."

Kate watched him go out and then sighed. Now she went over to the wall, took down a small, close-fitting hat of straw and pinned it on. She stepped out onto the plankwalk now, heading for the livery where she stabled her horse and buggy each day. Even the sunny May morning could not raise her spirits, as she walked down to the corner and crossed the busy street heading toward the livery stable.

While she waited for the hostler to hitch up the buggy, she thought of Giff Ballew almost with hatred. Things had been peaceful and time had cooled the old furies and had begun to dim memory. Now Ballew had come in and would surely break the tenuous truce. She tried to remember the Ballews and could not, since she would have been five when they left. Nor could she remember anything of the trial, although she had heard her father say often enough that Tom Ballew, while believing the South had a right to secede, had never preached sedition. It had been her father's belief that the poor and struggling farmers and cattlemen, jealous of Ballew's holdings, had denounced him as a rebel so that the government would seize his lands. It was Weybright who, in those poor times, had come up with the money to buy them and the toughness to hold them.

The hostler came up with the horse and buggy, handed her in and Kate drove to the corner, turned and headed out of town. She wondered if Ballew would go directly to her father, and she supposed he would. He seemed a headlong, reckless person; for him to think was to act, she supposed. From the little she had seen of him she thought how like the Weybrights he was. They were headstrong, stubborn, always wanted their way and usually got it. She could see nothing but trouble ahead.

The warm wind in her face was pleasant and the only cloud in the sky was a ragged wind-blown pennant over the San Dimas range to the west. The rolling country around her was becoming a pale green with the new grass and the cows with their newborn calves moved slowly away from the road at her approach. Her father, she knew, would be surprised at her early return but it wouldn't take long for him to find out her reason, she thought grimly.

Presently, the road forked and she took the left-hand track, and within another ten minutes the towering cottonwoods that sheltered the Box K were in sight. As she drove into the barn lot she saw a strange horse standing at the tie-rail by the yard gate. She knew her hunch had been right.

Prudencio, one of her father's Spanish hands, was working in the open-air blacksmith's shop which was simply four posts with a roof abutting the pole corral. He dropped his work and came over to her as she reined in, a squat, cheerful, middle-aged man whose dark skin bespoke Indian blood.

"I won't need her any more today, Prudencio," Kate said as she handed him the reins.

He helped her down and Kate headed directly for the house. It was built of adobe, but instead of the customary flat roof, it had a pitched one. The huge old cottonwoods met above it and, in spite of the spaded flower beds in the small fenced in yard, it had the air of a working ranch. Off to the east, close to the creek, was the adobe bunkhouse where Prudencio and their two other hands lived.

Kate went through the gate and as she walked up to the veranda she saw her father and Giff Ballew, both seated, talking together. She took off her hat now and stepped up on the veranda which spread across the living-room wing of the house.

Both men rose from their chairs and now Kate looked carefully at her father. There was a kind of boyish excitement in his seamed face. He was not a tall man, but his wide shoulders and deep chest gave him the illusion of bigness. His pale, thick hair was matched in color by his mustaches and his wedge-shaped face was fresh shaven. His gray eyes held a warmth and tenderness as he looked at her. "How come you're home? Did Sam decide to go fishing?" he asked.

Kate came up and kissed him on the cheek. "We both had spring fever."

Her father turned to Giff and said, "Kate, this is—"

"We've met," Kate said shortly.

"That's right," her father said. "I forgot Giff stopped by the paper."

"Did he tell you why he's here?" Kate asked.

"Yes, he wants help."

"And you agreed to give it to him?"

Her father frowned. "Why, all I can, yes."

Kate walked over to an old rocker and sat down, and the two men sank back into their chairs.

"Just what help did you ask for, Mr. Ballew?" Kate said. She knew there was hostility in her tone because her father, watching her, had surprise in his eyes.

"Why, if I'm to take this business into court without a deed or a record of a deed I've got to prove some way that my father owned that land." Giff's voice was thoughtful, patient.

Kate's was brusque as she asked, "So my father goes into court and swears lots of things. That to his knowledge Weybright's range was owned by Tom Ballew. That it was taken from him through perjury. That you're Tom Ballew's son. That and more, I suppose."

Giff nodded warily and now Kate said flatly, "He won't do it, Mr. Ballew."

"Now Kate," her father began, but she recklessly rode him down.

"You don't know what you're asking, Mr. Ballew," Kate said angrily. "It's not as simple as you make it out."

"How's that?" Giff asked politely.

Kate took a deep breath and looked at her father. There was plain warning in his eyes, but she went on recklessly. "I don't know that this is any of your business, but I'll tell it so you'll know why." She paused. "My husband was named Dan Miles. He was a no-good man if one ever lived. One night in town he got drunk and picked a quarrel with Tucker Weybright, Lynch's oldest boy. It was over a woman, and I wasn't that woman." Memory made her voice bitter. "Dan picked the quarrel and pulled his gun. Tucker Weybright shot and killed him."

Now she looked at her father and saw that his face

was bleak with the memory. "Dad wanted revenge on the Weybrights. He still does. Don't you, Dad?"

Mike Keefer was silent, but he dipped his head once in bitter acknowledgment.

Kate continued, "But before Dad could move, old Lynch Weybright came here. He was sorry, genuinely sorry, that Tucker had killed Dan. I think he was sorry on my account because he had no love for Dad and Dad had none for him since he'd stolen our land." She paused. "Lynch wanted to do anything in his power to make up for what his son had done, even though it wasn't Tucker's fault."

Now she looked at her father. "This is the part Dad doesn't like to remember, but he's got to. We were poor then, far poorer than we are now. Lynch Weybright loaned Dad a sizable amount of money to clear this place of the debts Dan had saddled it with. We're still paying back that money a little at a time." She leaned forward now. "Do you think Dad can get up on the witness stand and testify in your behalf? Lynch Weybright has our note that is long overdue. We anger him and we're through."

"Right is right," Mike Keefer said abruptly. "Lynch Weybright is a crook! Ballew proved that today."

"He may be a crook, but we're at his mercy," Kate said flatly. "When we've paid him the money we owe then you can indulge yourself in the luxury of calling him one, Dad. Now you can't." She looked at Ballew. "Surely you can understand this."

"I can," Giff said quietly. "If I'd known this, I wouldn't have asked." He rose now. "Was Bohanan the name of the man in the next county—the man that was a witness for my father?"

Kate said drily, "What Sam didn't tell you is that Bohanan is a partner in a business with Weybright. That leaves you Seth Parry, who's Weybright's lawyer."

Giff said nothing and now Kate asked gently, "Why don't you give it up?"

Giff gave her a wondering look and then moved over to Keefer. "Sorry I bothered you," he said and held out his hand.

Keefer accepted it and said wryly, "I'm sorry it's the way it is. I would like to help you, son. Weybright has it coming to him and I hope you win, but as Kate says, it will have to be without me."

"It will be," Giff said. He nodded to Kate and moved off the veranda, tramping toward his horse. Kate watched his back and the thought suddenly came to her, *Why, it's never occurred to him that he won't win.*

Giff stepped into the saddle and headed out of the Box K the same way he had come. Kate Miles had pretty much spelled out what he was facing, although she hadn't said as much. With Mike Keefer unable to help him, with Bohanan a partner of Weybright and Parry the lawyer for Weybright, it was up to him alone, he thought bleakly. He supposed there were still some men around here who had testified against his father. They would be unwilling to help him and, of course, would reiterate that his father had borne arms against the Union.

Where was he to start? he wondered. He was one man against the combined Weybright-Stoughton families and their crews. Maybe Kate Miles was right. Why didn't he give it up? Justice was a thing few people ever received from life, so why shouldn't he accept this injustice and quit?

As soon as he had framed the thought he dismissed it. There must be a way and he would find it. Now he looked over to the west at the near San Dimas range. Its dun foothills lifted to black timber that almost reached the bare peaks. Over there lay his ranch.

Abruptly Giff knew what he was going to do. He couldn't fight a man he had never seen, and he wanted to see Lynch Weybright.

When he came to the fork of the road he turned south, and feeling hungry he reached in his saddlebag and brought out strips of jerky on which he began to gnaw. Now he gave his gray appraisal of all the errors he had committed today. The first was his going immediately to Parry with his story. He should have gone first to the courthouse and without stating his name or his errand asked to see the deed book. Instead, he had given Parry time to warn Weybright or the deputy and the page had disappeared. Well, it was done, he thought with a wry sense of guilt, and he put it from his mind.

As he rode on the land began to tilt into the foothills, and here the range was greener and the scattered cattle he saw, bearing the Circle W brand, seemed fatter. Was he on his own range? he wondered.

Presently, as the road climbed, he was in cedar and piñon country, and now the road began to lift to the rim of the mesa. He rested his bay before the climb and then urged him on. Presently he achieved the break in the rimrock and rode out onto a level bench thinly stippled with cedar. He was having his look at it when he heard the sharp near crack of a rifle. At the same instant a geyser of dust and splintered rock lifted in front of his bay and the startled horse reared.

Giff fought the horse down and then looked up. From a cedar to the left of the road ahead of him a man on foot appeared, his carbine held at ready. From the other side of the road another man stepped out from behind a piñon tree, a cocked six-gun leveled at him. Both men walked toward him now and Giff sat slack in the saddle, both hands in sight on the saddle horn. The man on the left, dressed in rough range clothes, was a lean man, tall, perhaps thirty, with an aquiline nose above a wide, almost lipless mouth, and Giff had the fleeting impression that he looked like someone he had seen recently.

As the man on the right approached, Giff saw that he was little more than a boy, perhaps eighteen, and, observing him, Giff knew these two were brothers. The boy had almost the same features as his brother, but they were more refined and so well proportioned that he was handsome. His dark eyes held a wariness and excitement.

Now the man with the rifle halted and said thinly, "Dad wondered if you wouldn't be along."

Giff frowned in puzzlement and then it came to him. "You're Weybright."

"That's right, Tucker." Now he looked at the boy who simply lifted his gun, which Giff noticed was cocked.

"What do you want with me?" Giff asked of Tucker.

A faint smile passed fleetingly over Tucker Weybright's dark face. "Want to tell him, Lee?" he asked without looking at the boy.

"Sure." To Giff, Lee said, "Turn around and ride out of here."

"The farther the better," Tucker said. "This time we didn't shoot at you. Next time we will."

Giff was silent a moment and then he folded his arms and leaned on the horn, thumbing back his hat. "What's worrying you?" he asked mildly. A quick anger came into Tucker's eyes and Giff said, still mildly, "I'm only one man."

Tucker asked flatly, "What do you want here?"

"To talk with your father."

"Talk or shoot?" Lee asked drily.

"Take my gun, then," Giff said.

Now Lee looked at his older brother. "What about it, Tuck?"

Tucker Weybright was frowning and Giff knew he was undecided. Giff said, "Look, I'll talk with him sometime. I'll stop him on the street in town or wait for him on the road. Why not talk with him now? He's home, isn't he?"

Tucker seemed to have made up his mind. He said, "Just this once. When you ride out of here it'll be for the last time. Now get his gun, Lee."

The younger Weybright came over and lifted Giff's six-gun from its holster.

"Go, ahead," Tucker said.

Chapter Two

GIFF RODE on, and looking back saw that the Weybrights were each heading for a horse hidden in the cedars. Presently, he heard them approach and they fell in on either side of him. Giff made no attempt at conversation, and the Weybright brothers were equally silent.

In less than a mile the piñons began to thin out and Giff could see ahead of him a two-story log building butted up against the base of a rocky bench. A log bunkhouse lay to the west of the house and the tangle of the corrals and sheds was beyond it.

Giff recognized the bunkhouse as his first home. The big house was new and the trees that his father had planted were gone. Either they had been allowed to die or they had been chopped down. The place seemed to have never known a woman. There were no curtains at the windows of the house and nothing grew in the hard-packed yard. It was a man's place, the world of working cattlemen.

As they approached the barn lot, a man swung open the gate of a high corral and then, catching sight of them, halted. He had a coiled rope in his hand and now he shrugged it over his shoulder, shut the corral gate and then turned, waiting. Approaching him, Giff felt the sudden shock of recognition. This was the man, tall, straight, with white hair and white mustaches, that he had met on the courthouse steps this morning. This was why Tucker's face seemed faintly familiar. Giff knew now that Weybright had barely beat him to the courthouse.

The three of them reined up and now Lynch Weybright looked at his boys. "I thought I told you to run him off."

"He wanted to talk with you," Tucker said.

Now Lynch Weybright looked at Giff, his pale eyes fierce and proud. "I've got nothing to say to you, Ballew."

"Maybe you have, at that," Giff said. He swung out of the saddle and the two brothers were quick to dismount and come up beside him.

"Funny, I don't remember you," Giff said slowly.

"You and your rebel-loving father had left before we came," Weybright said curtly. "Now, what is it you want?"

"Just to hear you admit that this land is legally mine."

"Of course it is," Lynch said flatly. "What's that got to do with my keeping it?"

Giff tried to hide his amazement. "You admit I'm the owner?"

"I do not. I'm the owner. I said it's legally yours. Can you take it through the courts or by force?"

"I'm going to try."

"I understand you've got no deed at all. There's no record of your father ever owning it."

"Not after you got to the deed book there isn't. You did get to it, didn't you?"

"In time," Lynch said.

"And Parry got to you with my story, didn't he?"

"In time," the old man repeated. "That's what I pay him for. Why didn't you try to bribe him? I do."

Giff was silent, collecting his wits. Here Weybright

had admitted Giff's legal claim to this land. He also admitted to destroying the evidence on which any legal claim could be based.

Giff said slowly, "I take it you won't admit this in court."

"I'll deny I ever said it. So will my boys." He hooked his thumbs in his belt and said, "Go home, son. I don't want to hurt you, but I'm not going to let you hurt me." He looked around him. "I bought this place from the government. I fought thirty men for five years to hold it. I've put seventeen years' work in it. If you think I'm going to turn it back to the son of a rebel, think again." Now he looked at Giff. "There's nothing you can do to me. You've got no proof of past ownership. You can't take it from me, and if you try there are twenty men who'll gun you down."

"You're not one of the men who testified against my father, are you?"

"I did not. But I considered him a damn' rebel and he got what he deserved."

Giff felt a faint surge of anger and then it subsided. Arguing with the old man about his father's guilt was senseless, and would only bring him a beating. Still, the bland gall of Weybright rankled him and he wanted more than anything else to stir Weybright's temper. Now he turned slowly and looked at the house and the cook shack. Then he said mildly, "When I move in here I'm going to replant the trees my father put in."

When he looked back at the old man he saw the flush of anger creeping into his face and he knew he had succeeded.

Weybright said grimly, "The day you move in here will be the day of your funeral. I'll give you ground enough for a grave." Now his glance shuttled to his youngest son. "Lee, give me a hand. Tucker, take this man to our line and tell him not to come back."

Giff mounted and Tucker Weybright stepped into the saddle. Lee came over to his brother and handed him Giff's gun which he rammed in his belt. Giff kneed his horse around and Tucker, saying nothing, pulled in beside him on his left. They traveled the road in silence, and finally when they reached the cedars again Giff reined up and turned in his saddle for a last look at his boyhood home. It came to him then that this was a near hopeless situation. Lynch Weybright was confident enough of his strength that he could openly admit he was wrong and dare Giff to do something about it. It was, Giff admitted wryly, a pretty safe dare at the moment.

Tucker Weybright's voice interrupted his thoughts. "Take a good look at it, you joker, because you'll never see it again. If you try I'll drag you to our line with a rope."

Giff turned and put his horse into motion, fresh anger coming to him. He could take the old man's insolence because through strength and craftiness the old man had earned the right to be insolent. This son, however, would not let the old man's words stand. He wanted to rub some of his own salt into the wound.

"Sure, you're tough," Giff said drily. "There's nobody better when it comes to shooting drunks."

He saw a wild temper flare in Tucker's eyes and he jibed, "Go ahead and shoot. I haven't got a gun."

Tucker reined in and Giff saw that he was white around the mouth. With his left hand Tucker pulled Giff's gun from his waistband and tossed it to the ground ahead of his horse. "You've got one now," he said thinly.

Tucker's horse was a little ahead of his own, and now Giff nodded and casually stepped out of the saddle as if to accept the challenge. Then, not moving especially fast, he grasped Weybright's right stirrup with both hands and heaved mightily. Weybright, as Giff had anticipated, did not go for his gun, but instead made a grab for his saddle horn. It was too late, for by that time he was far off balance and falling.

Giff ducked under the belly of Weybright's horse as Weybright hit the ground, and then Giff lunged atop him, straddling him. Weybright was on his side and now Giff drove a blow into Weybright's jaw that sent a shock of pain clear to his shoulder. Weybright, swinging wildly, rolled over on his back and now he raised both hands and clawed at Giff's neck, trying to choke him. Giff tried to bat his hands away, but Weybright had grasped his yellow neckerchief with one fist and was now twisting it, trying to throttle him.

Holding his breath, Giff methodically slugged Weybright in the face, but the hold on his neckerchief did not loosen. Giff suddenly knew that if he did not break Weybright's hold he would be choked into unconsciousness. He heaved himself to his feet and kicked Weybright in the side, and now Weybright's instinctive reflexes ripped the neckerchief loose. Giff heard it tear and he drew in a blessed gust of air into his lungs. Now Weybright rolled over on his side, clawing at his gun, and Giff kicked his hand. Weybright rolled over, came to his knees and was almost erect when Giff lunged into him, his hand reaching for Weybright's gun. When he had it, he yanked it loose and dropped it and now Weybright was wholly on his feet, his right hand numbed from Giff's kick, hanging unclenched at his side.

Giff put the whole rolling weight of his body behind the fist that he drove into Weybright's belly and he heard Weybright's quick explosion of breath. Weybright's jackknife of pain brought his jaw down hard atop Giff's shoulder and Giff moved aside. He took a second to brace himself as Weybright wrapped his arms around his belly, leaving his face exposed. Now Giff moved in with a crossing right that caught Weybright on his shelving jaw. Weybright pivoted on the heel of his boot; he was unconscious before he fell face down in the dust of the road. He lay utterly still.

Giff drew in great reaching breaths of air as he watched Weybright. Now he moved over, picked up Weybright's gun and sailed it into the brush. As he tramped toward his own gun he saw his neckerchief torn in half on the ground, and he ignored it. When he had holstered his gun he came back to Weybright's horse, gave him a cut across the rump and watched him circle out in the brush and head for home. Stepping over Weybright, Giff mounted and put his horse in motion. This fight didn't amount to much, Giff knew, but it gave him a bitter satisfaction. Also, he knew bleakly, it made him fair game for retaliation from any of the twenty hands old Lynch had claimed.

Sam Furman had a decision to make and he knew he must make it himself. Tomorrow was press day and right now he should be rounding up and setting up the last of the ads and assembling the latest in local news. Instead, he was moping around the front office not really working at anything except at avoiding a decision.

Kate Miles was in the process of housecleaning the untidy desk and she watched Sam covertly as he poked in drawers and occasionally went to the window and stared out at the roof line across the street.

Presently, when she could not stand it any longer, Kate said, "Something troubling you, Sam?"

Sam started, and a feeling of guilt came upon him like a clap on the shoulder. He turned. "No more than usual, Katie. Why?"

"You should be busy."

Sam turned to the window. "Quit nagging. I'm not your husband."

"You're a poor actor, Sam. Yesterday you went charging off to the courthouse breathing fire. The last I heard you were shouting about the rights of men, sacredness of property, and all those noble sentiments. What cooled you down?"

Sam turned, almost angrily, but when he saw Kate watching him, a faint smile on her wide lips, the anger drained from him and in its place came a sheepishness. "I guess I got scared."

"Was the page missing?"

Sam dipped his head in the affirmative.

"Weybright took it, of course," Kate said.

Sam turned from the window, rammed his hands in his hip pockets and began to pace the room. "I would reckon so, but I wonder when. Ten years ago or yesterday?"

"Why, does it matter?"

Sam halted and looked at her. "I'm just trying to justify not doing anything about it," Sam said bitterly. "If it was cut out ten years ago, it certainly couldn't be classed as this week's news. If it was cut out yesterday, I suppose it would."

"Have we got to print all the news in this paper?" Kate said impatiently. "You never printed the time Sheriff Corbett arrested you for being drunk and disorderly."

"That's different," Sam said. "I'm not public news."

"This missing page isn't public news either!" Kate said hotly. "It affects two people. It's gone. What can you gain by printing that fact?"

"Look," Sam said flatly, "will you stop thinking like a woman? The deed book is a record of legal transactions. It shouldn't be altered or destroyed."

"You're being silly," Kate said. "What if a deed book in some county courthouse was destroyed in a fire? The world wouldn't end."

"Ah-h," Sam said in disgust. He moved back into the shop now, his hands still in his hip pockets and halted before the composing stone.

Kate followed and now she said quietly, "Suppose you print it, Sam. What do you suppose will happen?"

"Well, it won't do much good to announce the bare fact that it's missing. I would have to say the Ellice-Ballew deed was recorded on it. That'll point only to the Weybrights."

"Answer my question."

"I'm trying to!" Sam said impatiently. "Either Tucker or Lynch Weybright—not Lee, he's too young—will come in. I'll likely get pistol-whipped unless I can get a gun on them first. That won't settle anything. They'll just wait for me on a dark street."

"You said it all right there," Kate said drily.

"But I'm a damn' coward!" Sam shouted. "I know what I ought to do and I know the right thing to do. I'm just scared."

Kate ignored this. "Why don't you go on? What would you do after they pistol-whipped you?"

Sam thought a moment. "Demand action against whoever cut out the missing page."

"Then what would happen?"

Sam was silent.

"Who saw the page taken?" Kate prodded. "Did anyone see Weybright take it? Did they see him destroy it?"

"I think someone might have seen it."

"Larson? Barnard? You think they won't perjure themselves? They've already been paid money to, I imagine. But go on with your fairy tale, Sam. What happens if Weybright is called into court?"

"It'll make a lot of people happy."

"That's just it," Kate said angrily. "Weybright will lie, Larson will lie, Barnard will lie. Then half the county will come forward and lie that they saw Weybright take the page. They've been waiting twelve years to get even with the Weybrights! What's truth, when you can have revenge?"

Sam had no answer.

"You know what's going to happen if you print it, Sam? It won't take this Ballew long to find out Weybright's killer crew shoved a dozen families off Circle W. It won't take him long to find out their names. Breverton Breaks is full of them and their families. It won't take him much longer to convince them this is the time to even the score."

"He already knows about the old fight. I told him."

Kate looked at him a long moment. "Why did you?"

"How else could I explain why you walked away from him when he mentioned seeing your father? I told him you didn't want to see this fight start all over again."

Kate said bitterly, "So you give him the ammunition he needs. You print there's a page missing from the deed book. It points to Weybright. They always thought he was a crook and this proves it. Good. Let's choose up sides like we did before, get behind Ballew, and open the ball." Her voice turned sarcastic. "How they'd love this in Carmody's Saloon and in Dry Wells and Breverton Breaks. You can make it possible."

"Why shouldn't I?" Sam flared. "We've lived on our knees around here long enough! Weybright and Stoughton run the county! Their boy is sheriff! They can alter or destroy records and then bully us all into keeping quiet."

Kate said just as hotly, "I haven't any love for the Weybrights and Stoughtons, but they're better than the people Ballew will raise against them. Look at that saloon bunch and the Breaks bunch. Riffraff white trash. They drink all day and steal horses and cattle all night. They live in pigsties and have a new baby a year that they can't feed. They're intermarried and inbred and there isn't a one of them that's worth anything. All of them or their families were kicked off Circle W. This is Ballew's army and you're the recruiter if you print this!"

"Your family was kicked off," Sam countered hotly.

"And the daughter in our family—me—married the trashiest one of them all! But you don't recruit me! Or my father!"

Suddenly Sam smiled. "Katie, you make any cowardice seem reasonable and beautiful." He paused. "Speaking of beautiful, that's what you are when you're mad. Now cool off and tell me you'll marry me."

Kate shook her head once. "Back off, Sam, and don't change the subject."

Sam said wearily, "We've wrung that out enough, Kate. I guess I'll swallow my pride and my half ounce of courage and keep quiet." He added wryly, "But the next time I see Ballew I'll keep looking at his shirt pocket."

"What does that mean?"

"You don't think I can look him in the eye, do you?"

Todd Stoughton's Bib S adjoined Circle W. Weybright's buildings were of log, but the Bib S buildings were mostly adobe. Where Weybright had bought foothill country, his sister Myra and her husband had chosen the flats. Although the two home ranches were only three miles apart, they were so unlike in appearance and range that they might have been in separate territories. The two families were close to each other and clannish, and their crews seemed almost interchangeable to the people of this country.

This morning Lynch Weybright, as straight in the saddle as he was afoot, rode in silence alongside a

Spanish hand whose horse was branded Bib S. While old Lynch could speak fluent Spanish, he saw no reason for conversation. Ahead of him he could see the low sprawling main house of Bib S almost encircled by cottonwoods. The house, however, did not command his attention. There was a small knot of men in front of an open-face shed which was the Bib S blacksmith shop adjoining the big series of pole corrals. Approaching closer, he could see that one man was sitting with his back against the shed wall. Two Bib S hands were standing beside him. Myra and her husband stood aside from the trio, talking. Lynch observed a fresh cowhide had been thrown over the corral poles. Three saddled horses stood by the big metal trough that was half in and half out of the main corral. The mid-morning breeze stirred the leafing cottonwood and sent a plume of dust skittering across the barn lot.

Looking toward the seated man, Lynch asked his companion, "Did you say Faye Olmsted or Harvey?"

"He's Faye Olmsted," the Bib S rider replied.

Now Todd and Myra Stoughton moved toward the approaching pair. Todd Stoughton was in his sixties, a dry, taciturn, and ineffectual man who, even in high-heel halfboots, was shorter than his wife. His range clothes were clean and neat, almost dandified. Myra Stoughton had her brother Lynch's rangy build. She was a homely woman with a long face, and her gray hair was stuffed into a battered hat. This morning she wore a divided skirt and a man's duck jacket.

"Morning, Myra, Todd," Lynch said as he reined in. His glance lifted beyond them to the seated man. "Where'd they come across him?"

"One of those box canyons along the edge of the Breaks," Myra said. She and Lynch looked at each other significantly.

Now Lynch dismounted, brushed past his sister and headed for the seated man. Lynch knew him as one of the unwashed, shiftless riffraff who hung out on mean spreads over in the Breaks. He was a middle-aged man, unshaven, unnecessarily dirty, and his face had a furtive and sullen expression on it. Lynch halted before him.

"Get up," Weybright said peremptorily.

"They told me to sit down," Olmsted said.

"I'm telling you to get up," Weybright said sharply.

Olmsted came to his feet, and now Weybright observed almost mildly, "I understand Myra's hands caught you butchering out a steer of mine."

Olmsted said nothing.

"Well, I could turn you over to Corbett or I could have you beat up. You got a choice."

Olmsted did not answer.

"I don't think I'll do either," Lynch corrected himself.

"I vote for the first,' Myra said. She and Todd had come up behind Lynch. "He was caught red-handed."

Lynch only shook his head and now he turned to Todd. "You got pencil and paper on you, Todd?"

Stoughton shook his head and spoke to one of the punchers standing by Olmsted. "Go up to the office, Hank, and rip a blank sheet out of the tally book. Bring a pencil too."

Hank moved off in the direction of the house and now Lynch said to the hand he had ridden in with, "Get the forge going, will you?"

The hand moved into the shed and started about the business of warming up the forge. Weybright turned and tramped over to where the three horses were tied by the watertrough. Talking the horse that was not branded Bib S, he led him away from the others and then regarded the horse, stepping back and circling him. It was a good horse, Lynch saw, and he thought how typical of these white trash. The roof could fall on their heads, the children could go unclothed and hungry, the wife could dress in flour sacking, but the man of the family was always well mounted. Maybe, Lynch thought drily, a man needed good tools to work with. This man's work, of course, was rustling.

Presently, the puncher who had been sent for the paper halted beside him and absently Lynch tucked the pencil and paper in his vest pocket. Now he headed back toward the blacksmith's shop, halted before Myra, and handed her the pencil and paper. "Make out a bill

of sale for him to sign, Myra. I doubt if he can write."
He paused. "You got an iron of mine here?"

At Myra's nod, Lynch moved into the shed and passed
along the wall on which several branding irons were
hanging from rusty nails. When he found the Circle W
iron, he moved over to the forge in which the coals were
now going and placed the iron over the hottest cherry-
glowing spot. He noted that Myra had come up to the
wall and, using a board for backing, was writing out the
bill of sale.

When Lynch saw that the iron was hot, he picked it
up, accepted the bill of sale from Myra and walked
over to Olmsted. Extending the paper, he said placidly,
"Sign it. It's a bill of sale for your horse."

"I ain't lettin' you steal no horse from me," Olmsted
said.

Lynch extended the paper, lifted the branding iron
and moved toward Olmsted. "I wouldn't mind you wearing my brand one bit. Although you're the sorriest
critter that'll ever wear it." He paused. "You got a
choice, take it."

Flattened against the shed, Olmsted looked at Weybright with pure hatred in his eyes. "I think you'd do
it, damn you!"

"I can promise you I will."

Slowly Olmsted reached for the paper and, lifting a
knee to use for a brace, signed the paper.

Weybright pocketed it and said mildly, "You're afoot.
Get out of here."

Mouthing obscenities Faye Olmsted headed out across
the sunlit barn lot. Home for him, Weybright knew, was
a good twelve miles. The town and a livery horse were
a solid eight.

"That was too easy, Lynch," Stoughton observed.

Myra only shook her head and Lynch could read no
meaning into the gesture. "Let's go get some coffee,"
she said.

Stoughton lingered a moment to give orders to his
men, and Myra and Lynch headed for the house. They
entered a large kitchen holding a big black stove at the

far end; in the center was a long, heavy table with flanking benches. Since the crew had a cook shack adjoining the bunkhouse, Lynch had always wondered what a woman did with all this space, all this stove, all these cupboards, just to rustle up grub for two.

Myra stirred the fire and pulled the coffeepot toward the front of the stove. She was busily rustling up cups when Stoughton entered.

Lynch, seated on one of the benches, had a scowl of preoccupation on his face and was absently drumming the table with his fingers. Now he looked up at Myra. "Anything strike you funny about where your men found Olmsted?"

Myra came over to the table with the cups. "Yes. Thieves usually take care to drive their stolen beef back into the Breaks before they butcher it out."

"Exactly," Lynch said grimly. "Seems like Olmsted didn't bother to hide it."

Myra went back to the stove for the coffeepot and Stoughton seated himself on the bench opposite Lynch.

Returning with the pot, Myra observed, "I'm glad you were home instead of Tucker."

Lynch swiveled his glance to her. "Why?"

"Tucker would have done a lot worse than take the man's horse and set him afoot."

"He deserved worse."

Holding the coffeepot poised over a cup, Myra said, in a voice of exasperation, "You won't understand what I'm trying to say, Lynch. Tucker is half the reason these small outfits are getting so cocky. In town he'll walk them off the sidewalk. He'll call them anything he can lay his tongue to. He'll trifle with their women and then laugh at them."

"He likes his way, that's a fact," Lynch admitted, and did not concede anything in the admission.

Myra poured their coffee, returned the pot to the stove and came back to sit on the bench. Folding her big hands before her, she said, "I've always got on with these small ranchers. I treat them with firmness and I treat their wives like you do a good servant. I punish them for stealing and I discourage their shiftlessness."

She paused. "That's a lot better than riding them, threatening them and treating them like scum the way you and Tucker do."

"Your way's not Tucker's way," Lynch said, and added, "nor mine."

"You can see where your way is getting you," Myra said drily. "There was some Bib S beef in that canyon, the men said. Why did Olmsted shoot yours and not ours?"

Lynch, watching his sister, shrugged.

"I can tell you, even if Todd won't." She paused. "Your hand's always too heavy, Lynch, since the fight. So is Tucker's. Maybe all these white trash aren't Giff Ballews who can give Tucker what was coming to him, but they can make life pretty miserable for the big out-fits."

This was the first allusion to the beating Tucker had received at Ballew's hands yesterday. Lynch didn't par-ticularly care who knew about it and he would never have tried to hide it from his sister. Still, it rankled him to hear it mentioned.

"That was just a lucky thing," he said in quiet arro-gance. "It won't happen again."

Stoughton spoke for the first time and in a mild tone of voice. "How do you aim to handle Ballew?"

Lynch snorted. "Why does he need handling? He's got no papers or record of papers. He's one man. Yester-day he surprised Tuck. He won't again. A good beating will move him out of the country." He added thought-fully, "I don't think it'll even take that."

Myra appeared to agree with this dismissal of Ballew, and Stoughton, by his silence, seemed to concur. They drank their coffee now, talking of range conditions, of a pair of springs that both outfits used which seemed to be drying up too early in the season.

When Lynch had finished his coffee, he rose and Myra rose with him. "Well, Lynch, you may be right about Tucker. I don't mind enemies, but I've never gone out of my way to make them. It works, and I wish you could get it through Tucker's head."

"He'll do it his way, Myra," Lynch said with an easy

confidence. "I won't be here forever. He's got to learn how to handle things his own way."

"Well, thank goodness, Lee's not that way."

Lynch clapped his Stetson over his thick white hair. "No," Lynch conceded slowly, "Lee's young. He's a little soft, but he'll shape up.' He looked at Myra, and as he smiled his white mustaches lifted faintly. "After all, he's a Weybright."

When Giff woke close to noon in his small room at the back corner of the hotel, he was surprised at the hour. He told himself that a week's hard riding and his brawl with Tucker Weybright had drawn on reserves which only sleep could replace. He knew, however, that this wasn't true. He had lain far into the morning because there was simply nothing else to do. A visit to the Circle W and the consequent fight with Tucker Weybright was an ending to something that had never really been started.

Down in the hotel dining room he ate quickly, bought a handful of cigars in the lobby, tucked all but one in his vest pocket and then moved out onto the veranda. Here he pulled up one of the wired barrel chairs, fired up his cigar, put his feet on the railing and regarded this sunny town with a grave distaste. Old Weybright had told him to get out of here. Maybe that was the best advice. Still, there must be, there had to be a flaw in Weybright's scheme, he thought as he watched the noon-hour crowd on the streets homing for the midday meal.

He smoked his cigar down and fired up another and still no plan of offense occurred to him. He wondered then, almost idly, just how much the Weybright family had increased Tom Ballew's holdings. If he were going to stay here until he got his rights he had better learn who his neighbors would be and how big their spreads were. In short, to understand the politics of this country that Sam Furman had hinted at, he should know all about the people and their ranches. The Land Office would be able to supply him with part of that information.

Accordingly, after the noon hour, he inquired where the Land Office was, and was told that it was in the basement of the courthouse. Reaching it, he found it was a dark, dim room, an open vault in its rear wall. Racked at the side wall behind the counter were stacks of plat books which would, of course, record the original patents on federal land to landowners.

An old man, almost frail, with sharp bleach eyes, was behind the counter. He had about him the old man smell of seldom-washed clothes and of indifference to cleanliness. Since the sign on the entrance door had said U.S. LAND OFFICE and in the lower corner had been painted RODNEY ALLEN, ASSISTANT REGISTER, Giff supposed this was Allen. It took him only a few minutes to discover that the old man was a talented reporter with a storehouse of local knowledge that was not contained in the plats he showed Giff.

During that long session Giff got an accurate picture of the land and landowners of the area. Weybright, for instance, had quadrupled the thousand acres of Ballew holdings and Stoughton matched him in acreage if not in cattle. To the south of the Stoughton holdings were the Breverton Breaks, a rough country which held numerous small plots of once irrigated land which was largely abandoned for farming now because of the uncertain water supply. Most of the families Weybright had kicked off had settled here. To the east of the Weybright-Stoughton holdings were small and middle-sized ranches like the Keefers'; too often they were marginal operations and had changed hands many times. North of Harmony there were middle-sized holdings along the San Dimas range, but they bordered the desert north of Harmony and traded with and shipped from the northern towns. There was only one company operation in the country and that lay far north beyond the desert.

As he listened to the old man the possibility of a plan came to Giff, and when Allen had finished Giff said, "Tell me more about these people in the Breaks. You say they're mostly families that Weybright pushed off Circle W?"

Allen nodded and then grimaced. "They're not much.

Most of them drifted out of the South so they wouldn't
have to fight. The men only work when they have to.
They run a few cull beef. Some try dry farming, and
others cut wild hay up in the mountains. They steal
when they can, and the big ranchers claim they're rustlers to a man. Corbett keeps a pretty sharp eye on them."

"They hold a grudge against Weybright?"

"They hate them, of course, but they're afraid of
them. That long fight took the heart out of them."

"Any kind of settlement out in the Breaks?"

The old man started to shake his head and then said,
"Dry Wells—if you could call it a settlement. It's a
stage stop, saloon, and eating place. A couple of houses."

Giff pushed away from the counter. "I've taken a lot
of your time. I don't suppose you'd close up this place
and let me buy you a drink."

"Try me," old Allen said.

Giff smiled and the old man reached for his hat which
was under the counter, put it on, closed his vault, came
out from behind the counter and gestured Giff through
the door, which he locked after them.

Once on the street Giff said, "You name the place. I'm
a stranger here."

"There's two saloons in town," old Allen said. "The
best one's the First Chance. Got a nice gambling layout.
Me, I don't have enough money to gamble, so I go to
Carmody's. I'm used to it."

"We'll make it Carmody's then." They crossed Main
Street in the bright sun, heading south, and as the
business buildings began to peter out, they came to a
one-story adobe building that didn't even boast a false
front or an identifying sign. The owner presumably
thought that the louvered half-doors would identify his
establishment. Giff noted a dozen or so ponies at the
tie-rail, before he followed old Allen into the dark and
narrow room.

The bar ran the length of the room on the right and
there were card games going at the two round, bare
tables that took up the rest of the room. A half-dozen
men were bellied up to the bar and in his one brief
glance Giff saw that these were men of a type. They were

roughly dressed and uniformly unshaven; Giff sensed that if he had not been in the company of old Allen, whom most of these men knew and nodded to, he would have been regarded with a quiet and surly suspicion.

The bar caught frail old Allen in mid-chest and when he put his elbows on the bar his arms were necessarily spread wide like a bird taking off. He crooked a finger and said to the burly, tall bartender in a soiled apron, "None of that Breverton bile, Joe. Give us good whiskey."

The bartender grinned amiably and now old Allen turned to Giff. "He brings in a special brand of Forty Rod for his customers. You could etch glass with it."

Giff was beginning to like this old boy and he wondered if he had been here during his father's time. He asked, "Do you remember Tom Ballew? He owned part of the Weybright place."

The old man's sharp eyes regarded him. "I wondered when you'd tell me who you are. No, I didn't know him, but I heard about you."

Giff said nothing.

"The sheriff seen you yet?"

Giff shook his head. "I haven't been hiding."

"He will. He doesn't like his courthouse shot up."

The drinks came. Old Allen tossed his off immediately and poured another. Giff nursed his drink and was wondering about the sheriff when the batwing doors slammed open and a roughly dressed puncher came slowly into the room. He was a little unsteady on his feet, Giff noted, and he wondered if the man was drunk.

The puncher, instead of coming up to the bar, sought the nearest chair and exhaustedly slacked into it.

"You've taken your time, Faye," one of the card players said. "Where you been?"

Olmsted didn't answer. Tiredly he reached down and began to pull off a boot, groaning and grimacing as he did so. When the boot came off the watchers saw that Faye's dirty foot was covered with blood. They watched while he took off his other boot and saw that this dirty foot was in the same condition.

"Your horse get away from you?" one of the card players asked.

"He got away all right," Olmsted said bitterly. Now he looked at the bartender. "Give me a pint and bring it here, will you, Joe? I'll take a pitcher of water too."

Olmsted looked about the room and Giff saw the wild anger smoldering in the man's eyes. Two of the players at the back card game rose and approached Olmsted. "How far you walk?" one of them asked.

"Eight-nine miles."

"Your horse throw you?" the second asked curiously.

Olmsted regarded him with bitterness. "He didn't throw me. He's in Weybright's corral right now."

One of the seated card players scowled and looked at his companion. "What's he doing there?"

"Weybright stole him!" Olmsted said flatly, angrily. His glance traveled around the room, paused briefly on Giff and then veered off. "I run into a Circle W steer this morning about sunup. He had a broken leg and was almost crazy with hurting. I put him out of his misery and then I figured I'd skin and gut it so's the meat would keep before I rode over to Lynch's."

A couple of men nodded and now Olmsted looked defiantly around the room before he continued. "A couple of Bib S riders come up on me. They thought I was stealing the steer. When I showed 'em the broken leg they claimed I did it when I was skinning it out. They took me over to the Bib S and sent for Lynch."

Again he paused and Giff, as well as every man in the room, read Olmsted's story as an admission that he had been caught stealing a Circle W beef. Joe the bartender had come around the mahogany and now he put a pint of red whiskey, a water glass, and a pitcher of water before Olmsted. The man did not bother to use the glass. He wrenched out the cork and took three long swallows from the bottle. Afterward, his eyes watering, he drank two glasses of water. Nobody said anything since they were waiting for the finish of his story.

Olmsted's voice was raised in fresh anger as he went on. "When Lynch got there the old buzzard heated up an iron, backed me up against the wall and threatened to brand me if I didn't sign a bill of sale to him for my horse. Then, by God, he put me afoot, and I hiked it here."

By this time every man in the room, save old Allen and Giff, were gathered around Olmsted's table. One man spoke up, "Hell, that's robbery."

The second said, "Sure. Who do you go to about it? Corbett?"

There was forced, wry laughter at this remark and now Olmsted said, "He won't get away with it! From now on I'll shoot every head of Circle W beef I run across. I try to do a man a favor and that's what I get."

"Old King Weybright," another man said sourly. "Makes his own laws and tells his own sheriff how to rule on 'em."

"There'll come a day," one of the card players said softly. He looked at Olmsted. "The trouble is, Faye, you're too neighborly."

"Was that damn' Tucker there?" someone asked.

"Not likely," a sour voice observed. "He'd of shot Faye in both legs before he put 'em afoot."

Now Giff looked at old Allen, who seemed to have lost interest in this. Perhaps he had been a witness to similar scenes before. "Another?" Giff asked.

"This'll do me," Allen said.

Giff paid and, following Allen, tramped out past Olmsted's audience onto the boardwalk.

They turned upstreet and now Giff asked, "Who was that Faye?"

"One of the Olmsted brothers," old Allen said. "That was the Breaks bunch in there. Sounds like the Bib S boys caught Faye hands down." He was silent a moment and then shook his head. "Lynch can be rough, but like that fellow said, Tucker can be rougher."

They parted at the corner and Giff, watching the old man across toward the hotel, felt a sudden gloom. Listening to the old man in the Land Office, he'd wondered if the Breaks families weren't his natural allies. They hated Weybright and had a grievance.

But after one look at the crowd in the saloon and listening to them comment on Faye Olmsted's story, he

knew this could never be. The whole seedy lot of them
were good only for an ambush at night, and that wasn't
the way he wanted to regain his rightful inheritance.
No, he must count them out.

Or must he? He kept remembering something old
Allen had said: *They steal when they can and the big
ranchers claim they're rustlers to a man.* For a still
minute he thought about this, then a faint smile lifted
the corner of his mouth.

Now he stepped into the street, waited for a wagon
to pass, achieved the far walk and tramped it until he
came to the door of the *San Dimas Times.* Without
pausing he palmed open the door and entered.

The room, although it had been tidied up since he
last saw it, was empty and he tramped through it back
into the dark shop. Sam Furman was working at the
composing stone while Kate Miles stood before the type
case, a stick in her left hand, expertly setting type.

Giff halted alongside Sam, who looked up now and
grinned. "Come to borrow my gun again?"

Giff shook his head. "I want to put an ad in your
paper. Is there time to get it in this week's issue?"

Sam nodded and tilted his head toward Kate. "Give
it to her."

Giff moved over to Kate who finished setting up a
stick of type before she looked up. Giff touched his hat
and said, "Sam said to give you my ad."

Kate nodded, took the stick of type over to Sam who
lifted the type out from the stick and placed it in the
forms. Kate returned with the stick and said, "All right,"
and waited, her expression noncommittal.

"I want in pretty big letters the words, 'The public
is invited'—" Giff said.

Swiftly, her hands darting to the compartments of the
type case, Kate placed the type in the stick, "The public
is invited," she echoed.

Giff went on: "—by the rightful owner of those lands
lying between the Bib S Ranch and the Mill Iron Ranch
and between Pine Creek and Walls Canyon—"

"Slow down," Kate said. Again, swiftly, she set the

type in the stick and then, looking at Giff, said, "You're in the middle of a sentence you know."

"I know," Giff said coldly, and he continued: "—to help themselves to all stock which now unlawfully encumbers aforesaid lands and which are being unlawfully trespassed upon."

Kate settled the stick on the case and looked closely at Giff. "Do you know what you're saying?"

"Yes." Giff's answer was cold. "I can say anything as long as I pay for it."

Wordlessly Kate finished setting up the ad and then walked over and laid the stick on the stone in front of Sam. "Read that, Sam."

The type on the stick was backward to Sam but long habit allowed him to read it swiftly. Finished, his jaw slacked a little and then his glance lifted to Giff. "That's a plain invitation to rustle Circle W beef."

"It was meant to be."

"And you'll lead your little army of rustlers, will you?" Kate demanded.

"I will not move a head of beef or ride with a man who moves one. If the owner won't move his cattle off my grass, maybe somebody else will." Giff's voice was almost unfriendly.

"That's it, Katie!" Sam said jubilantly. "I'm too much of a coward to do anything about the missing deed page, but I can print this. It's a paid ad and not a news item or an editorial, is it?"

"It's worse," Kate said in a tight voice.

Now Sam looked at Giff. "Thank you, my friend. I presume you want it signed Giff Ballew."

Giff nodded. "How much do I owe you?"

"Nothing," Sam said, and looked at Kate. "I'm the one who owes you."

Chapter Three

THE SAN DIMAS TIMES was printed on a Thursday morning and was usually in the post-office boxes of its subscribers by noon. On this Thursday it was the turn of Tucker and Lee Weybright to do the weekly errands in town for both the Circle W and the Bib S. Considering the wants of both crews and two families, Lee had a long list, and it was only when all the purchases were loaded in the buckboard that Lee stopped by the post office for the two ranches' mail. Tucker was around town.

Loading the mail in the gunnysack, he tramped down the plankwalk toward the buckboard which he had left just around the corner from the livery stable. He was whistling thinly until he reminded himself that Tucker, if he were here, would not approve. Tucker was always looking for trouble in town and he prepared for it with an excessive arrogance. Whistling implied that the whistler was carefree and Tucker would never want anyone to have that impresion of a Weybright. Lee stopped whistling.

He had thrown the sack of mail on the seat and had a boot on the wheel hub when he heard his name called. He looked across the street and then the call came again, "Oh, Lee."

He swiveled his head, looked up and saw Seth Parry, both hands on the sill of the open window of his second-story office.

"Can you come up a minute?" Parry called.

Lee moved past the team, ducked under the tie-rail and mounted the stairs two at a time. Parry was waiting for him in his office, and they shook hands, Lee a little awkwardly and with the uncertainty of his youth.

"I wondered if you'd seen this week's *Times?*" Parry asked then.

"I got it in the mail, but I haven't looked at it."

Parry gestured toward his desk. "Take a look at my copy." He straightened out the paper, leafed to the middle page, then pointed to an ad which announced in boldfaced type, **An Invitation to the Public.**

Lee read it through, frowning, and then read it through once more. Then he straightened and glanced at Parry. "Why, he's talking about Circle W."

"Exactly."

Lee was still frowning. "An invitation to the public to take our beef?"

Parry nodded.

"But he doesn't own the land. We do."

"He thinks he does and this is his way of striking back at your father." He paused. "Is Lynch in town?"

"No, but Tuck is."

"Then I'd advise you to tell Tucker and your father to be on the lookout. There is a certain element over south that will read this as an invitation to steal you blind. It was meant as such."

Frowning, Lee looked again at the ad and now anger came. "What're we going to do about this?" he demanded, tapping the paper.

"Ballew is claiming land that he can't prove in court is his," Parry said. "That's a matter for the courts. Still, you can't wait that long." He hesitated, frowning. "If I were your father I'd place an ad in the next issue of the *Times*. In it I would state I was the legal owner of this property and of all the stock grazing on it. I would further state that any one trespassing on this property and taking or receiving Circle W stock would be prosecuted to the full extent of the law."

"Where does that get us?" Lee asked angrily.

"It establishes your case in court if you catch anyone rustling your beef, or, what is more important, anyone receiving it."

Lee thought this over in silence, his handsome face immobile. He could see Parry's point. If the riffraff in the Breverton Breaks accepted Ballew's invitation, they would have to dispose of the Circle W beef they rustled. This ad that Parry proposed was plain warning to the public that if anyone accepted or purchased Circle W beef they could be arrested and jailed.

He nodded. "I'll tell Dad what you said. I reckon Dad would ask you to draw up the wording, so I'm asking you now."

"Be glad to," Parry said.

"Well—thanks, Mr. Parry," Lee said and he turned and went out.

Below, he backed his team and buckboard away from the tie-rail, crossed Main Street and then pulled up in front of Carmody's Saloon, the place Tuck had named where Lee was to pick him up. Lee knew, and didn't like it, that Tuck made a point of dropping in at Carmody's every time he was in town. It was a matter of pride with Tuck that he should be seen and heard in this hangout of the men who hated him. He wanted it known that he was contemptuous of these people and unafraid of them.

Lee reined in, rummaged around in the sack of mail until he found the *Times,* and then put it on the seat. Afterward he swung down, crossed the walk and shouldered through Carmody's batwing doors, halting just inside them. There were a half-dozen men at the far end of the bar. Tucker, standing in quiet arrogance, had the rest of the bar to himself.

When he saw Lee he straightened up, slapped a coin

on the counter and moved toward the door. Lee went out ahead of him, but instead of climbing into the buckboard, Lee reached for the copy of the *Times* on the seat and opened it.

Tucker came up to the side and said, "What you got, Lee?"

Silently, Lee handed him the newspaper and pointed to the bold advertisement.

Tucker read it slowly and only once, and when he looked up at Lee his pale eyes were blazing. "So he thinks he'll get away with that, does he?" Tucker said thinly. For a moment he stood irresolute, then he handed the paper to Lee, turned and went back into the saloon.

Lee, standing beside the buckboard, heard Tucker's wrathful and bitter voice as it came from the saloon. It said: "If any of you white trash accept that invitation of Ballew's, you're dead, your families are burned out and moved. Pass the word around out at Dry Wells."

Now Tucker came out of the saloon and halted by Lee. "Where's this Ballew hang out?"

Lee strugged.

"Come on," Tucker said curtly. He angled across the street, Lee beside him, rounded the corner of the hotel, mounted the steps and crosed the lobby to the desk where a middle-aged clerk was sorting mail.

"You got a Giff Ballew registered here?" Tucker demanded.

The clerk looked up. "Did have. He checked out this morning."

The southbound stage passed Giff just as he was entering the Breverton Breaks and he reined up to let the pluming dust settle. The dust reminded him that he had forgotten to buy a new neckerchief to replace the one Tucker Weybright had torn off him in their fight.

Pushing on down the gentle grade into the Breaks, Giff looked at the country around him. It was almost a badlands of clay dunes holding isolated pockets of only fair grazing. The few cattle he saw, he guessed were culls bought from the more prosperous ranches at shipping time. He passed two abandoned farms whose only crops were fields of waist-high tumbleweed. Deeper in the Breaks there were several handkerchiefed-sized farms, but in all this day's ride he saw nothing that resembled a prosperous working ranch. He thought with a grim satisfaction that his advertisement in the *Times* might hold a bitter appeal to the men of this sorry country. He wanted to see if it did.

Dry Wells, a nine-hour ride from Harmony, was announced by a stand of cottonwoods and, as Giff approached it, he thought that it suited the country. A tangle of cedar-pole corrals abutted a bare dune, and a long adobe building under the cottonwoods was the stage station and bar. Two smaller single-room adobe buildings lay between the station and the corrals. A sorry looking team hitched to a buckboard and two saddle horses were tied in front of the saloon.

Giff dismounted, stiff from the long ride, and tramped toward the open door above which was a paint-peeled sign that said BAR. The B had been painted backward, Giff noted.

He stepped into a dark, dirt-floored room, hearing conversation die, and as the sunlight washed out of his eyes he saw there was a rough deal bar on his right at which three men were standing. The bartender was a huge man. He wore no shirt over his dirty underwear and Giff saw that his left hand was missing. A horse-blanket pin closed the cuff of the left sleeve of the underwear. Broad and greasy galluses held up his pants. At the far end of the room canned goods and bottles were racked in a sorry display.

Under the stares of the three customers Giff moved over to the bar, thumbed his hat off his forehead and asked for whiskey. He could see that the three men had a paper open on the bar before them and Giff guessed that the stage which had preceded him had delivered this week's copy of the *Times*.

The bartender set out a shot glass and bottle for him, and Giff slowly poured a drink. He heard one of the men say quietly, "If anybody moves in, don't think I won't get my share."

The second said, "Who you reckon this Ballew is?"

The first man shrugged and said, "It says right here he owns it and that Weybright is trespassing."

The bartender, who was leaning against the back bar and who had tucked his left arm under his galluse, now observed in a rasping voice, "If Weybright misses any beef, where you think he'll look first?"

"Let him look," one man said. "It won't be the first time."

Giff put a coin on the counter and said, "Can a man get something to eat here?"

"If the stage bunch didn't clean us out," the bartender said curtly. He walked to the door in the wall at the end of the bar and called, "Hannah, got any grub left?" Then he turned to Giff and gestured with his head, "Go on in."

Giff moved through the door into a bare room holding only a long table and benches on either side of it. He heard one of the bar customers leave the room behind him. A girl, perhaps twenty-five, rose from a bench as he entered and gave him a glance of complete indifference. She was a pretty girl with black curly hair and full, almost sullen, lips. Under the blouse and skirt which was protected by an apron, Giff saw that she was a full-bodied woman and thoroughly conscious of it. Then she moved into the kitchen out of his sight.

She, too, had had a copy of the *Times* spread out on the table before her.

Giff laid his hat on the bench and sat down at the place the girl had vacated. He had overheard just enough in the bar to know his notice had created a live interest. However, he knew that any attempt at conversation with these men would be met with a taciturn silence. He wondered if Hannah would be more open. Now he could hear her talking briefly to someone in the kitchen.

In a few minutes Hannah returned with a tin plate of warmed-up steaks and a mound of fried potatoes. In her other hand she carried a cup of coffee and a knife and fork. As she set them on the table Giff looked up at her and tapped the ad. "This is new country to me," he said slowly, "but does this happen often around here?"

Surprisingly the corner of the girl's full mouth lifted
in a faint smile. "This is the first time and I think it'll
be the last."

"Whoever this fellow is, he's inviting everybody to
rustle somebody else's stock."

"You can bet the invitation will be accepted," Hannah
said drily.

"Whose stock will be rustled?"

"The Weybrights', Circle W."

Giff frowned. "They big enough to stop it?"

"Big enough and mean enough," Hannah said.

Giff pushed the paper aside and began eating. Hannah
pulled out the opposite bench and sat down.

Giff said abruptly, "How did your husband lose his
hand?"

Hannah said quietly, "He's not my husband."

Giff speared a piece of meat, raised it halfway to his
mouth and paused. "You mean you work here because
you want to?"

Before the girl could answer a dark-haired little girl
in a clean dress and bare feet came into the dining room,
circled the table, halted by Hannah and turned her back
to the woman saying, "Button me up, Mommie."

Hannah buttoned up the little girl's dress, smacked
her on the bottom and said, "Run out and play and
stay out of the bar."

Now the little girl turned and gravely surveyed Giff
for a curious moment. In the few seconds he studied her
features, it came to him with sudden shock that he was
familiar with the straight mouth, the aquiline nose, the
deep-set pale eyes. This was a Weybright face. He
glanced swiftly at Hannah who was watching him.

The little girl went back into the kitchen and now
Hannah looked levelly at Giff. "Does that answer your
question?" she said drily. "I work here because I have
to. Don't tell me I'm too pretty to be in this hole."

"I take it you've heard that before."

"I have, so don't you push it. Her father's still
around."

Giff nodded. "I've met him."

Hannah watched him a still moment and then she announced, "You're Giff Ballew, aren't you?'"

Giff ceased eating and studied her a moment. "Are you guessing, or do you know?"

Hannah smiled crookedly. "In this country we're pretty careful about watching brands. The hostler in town picked yours up the first day."

Giff went on eating, now feeling somewhat foolish. Of course, the man who had left the bar as he came in here had spotted his horse, circled back to the kitchen and told Hannah. It even could be that the stage driver had reported his approach hours before. This was a careful country, Giff thought grimly.

His reflections were interrupted by Hannah's voice, which was dry and faintly unfriendly. "You don't mind taking chances, do you?"

Giff looked up. "I don't, but why do you say that?"

Hannah gestured toward the paper. "How did you know there wouldn't be Circle W riders in the bar? They come here, you know."

"Looking for stolen stock?"

"That, too," Hannah nodded.

Giff finished the last of his potatoes, took a drink of coffee, drew out a cigar and fired it up, then he put both elbows on the table, looked carefully at his cigar and then lifted his glance at Hannah. "Does Tucker keep you here as a spy?"

He saw the anger come into Hannah's eyes and saw her face darken. "There are three Weybrights. Why Tucker?"

"I'm guessing either of the other two would have married you and given you a home. At least they would have done better by you than this."

"What did you come out here for?" Hannah said angrily. "Not just to bully me."

Giff shook his head. "No, I wanted a look at this country and the men in it. I wanted to see how hungry they are."

"I was raised in it. I can answer that. They're hungry and always have been. They'll steal anything. Sometimes just for the fun of it." She paused and said bitterly,

"They're easy to hate." She shook her head and continued. "I've got a father, mother, brothers, and sisters over west five miles. It's been four years since any one of them has spoken to me."

Giff said abruptly, irrelevantly, "Suppose my newspaper invitation was accepted. Is there any way these people could get rid of the stuff?"

Hannah eyed him coldly. "If I told Tucker the ways there are, I don't think I'd be here."

"But you won't."

Hannah shook her head. "No, because I'm one of these people. Tucker took me for an ignorant white-trash girl, so with him I'm going to stay that way. I'd already chosen sides when I was carrying his baby. I'm for these people and against him even if he pays Kelsey to keep me here."

Giff drank the last of his coffee, slid the bench back and stood up. Hannah rose too. As Giff picked up his hat Hannah said, "You pay at the bar."

Giff nodded and headed for the bar when Hannah said quietly, "One more thing, Ballew. Are you planning to ride the back trails?"

"I hadn't thought about it," Giff said slowly.

"Then you'd better start thinking." Hannah's voice held warning. "Tucker hasn't told me this, but I've seen him work it. When he wants a man he'll take a couple of his toughest hands off ranch work. He'll put them on the trail of the man he wants. They do nothing else but hunt. Sometimes it takes them weeks, sometimes months, but they get their man. One hand acts as a relay for fresh horses."

Giff thought this over a moment and then said, "What if I don't run?"

"You'd better. Otherwise, all it takes is a dark street in town and a lying witness to say you started it. He's got two crews to draw from for that witness." She paused. "He'll pick up your trail here by nightfall."

"Who from?"

She nodded toward the bar. "He's got Kelsey in his pocket right now. The message is already on its way to Circle W."

Giff studied her a moment then asked curiously, "Why are you telling me all this?"

Hannah hesitated a long moment and then she shrugged. "Something in my head maybe. I'm Tucker's woman whether he marries me or not, but I hate his ways and all he stands for. I'd like to see him stomped." She added soberly, "Does that make sense?"

"To a woman, maybe," Giff conceded, and he tramped out.

When Kate drove the buggy into the barn lot that evening Prudencio was waiting as usual to accept the reins and help her down. She scooped up some mail and the paper from the seat, then headed for the kitchen door.

Sarita, Prudencio's wife, was standing just outside the kitchen door. She was a small, plump, graying woman and there was plain solicitude in her dark eyes as she watched Kate approach.

"You look tired, Mrs. Miles," was her greeting.

Kate smiled faintly. "Busy day, Sarita."

"Everything is in the oven and ready."

"Fine, you run along and get Prudencio's supper," Kate said. She moved into the small kitchen where places for two were set on the oilcloth-covered table in the middle of the room. Depositing the mail on top of the table, she took off her hat which she hung on a hook behind the door and then moved across the kitchen to the big black stove.

She was tired, she thought, and she wondered why. This day had really been no busier than any other press day. Then she thought she knew. Ever since Sam had directed her to accept Giff Ballew's advertisement an apprehension had settled on her that she could not shake. Ballew had been foolish and Sam even more foolish. Both, she knew, were flirting with disaster.

As she was looking in the oven to see what Sarita had prepared for their supper, her father came into the room from the barn lot. He sailed his hat into the rocking chair by the window, asking mockingly, "How's the lady editor?" as he patted her on the shoulder on his way to the sink. He pumped himself a basin of water and washed his hands.

"What did you do today, Dad?" Kate asked.

Mike Keefer snorted. "Put a box in that spring at Red Butte. Wouldn't surprise me if I cut off all the water."

He moved over to the table, picked up the paper, lifted his hat from the rocker, dropped it on the floor and sank into the chair with a sigh. "What's doing in town?"

"It's all in the *Times*," Kate said tonelessly.

She busied herself preparing supper and her father began to read the paper. Dusk was settling and now Kate took the lamp from its wall shelf, put it on the table and lighted it. Covertly she watched her father as he leafed over to the second page. Ballew's advertisement was in such bold type that she knew it would attract his attention instantly.

Presently she saw him frown and then he gave a great explosive laugh. "Good! Good!" he said delightedly, and now he glanced up at Kate. "That Ballew is a slick one."

"He'll be a sick one pretty soon," Kate said tartly.

"What he says is right. Weybright is trespassing," Keefer insisted.

"That's got nothing to do with it, Dad. Just what do you think will happen now?"

"I think a lot of these small boys will start whittling him down, that's what."

"Exactly." Kate's voice was sharp in exasperation. "Now will be the time when everybody gets even with everybody else."

Keefer slowly stroked his mustache with the back of a finger and regarded Kate, who was standing stiffly by the table. "How do you figure that?"

"Has anyone in that Breaks bunch or Carmody's Saloon crew got a grudge against you?"

Keefer scowled. "What's that got to do with this?"

"Go on! Answer me," Kate jibed.

"Yes," Keefer said. "I've had trouble with the Wallings ever since I fired Ben."

"All right. What's to prevent the Wallings from pushing Circle W stuff on to our range? Old Lynch would think we had accepted Ballew's invitation. There'd be more bad blood between us. What's to prevent anybody with a grudge from getting even with an enemy?" Kate shook her head. "All Ballew has done with that ad is to wipe out the law."

"I don't see that," Keefer said.

"Some man takes Ballew at his word and steals Circle W beef. Lynch and his boys retaliate. Friends of the man strike back. You think Corbett can control Lynch and his boys? Do you think he'll even want to?"

Her father was silent a moment. "No," he answered grudgingly.

"Then I've got a good notion about what you should do, Dad."

"What I should do? I'm not in this."

Kate went on adamantly. "Go over to Circle W and tell Lynch how this looks to you. Tell him you're in sympathy with him and you'll help any way you can."

"But I'm not, and I won't!" her father said flatly. "I won't rustle his beef, and that's as far as I'll go."

Kate moved over to the stove. "He'll think the whole world is his enemy, Dad. He'll suspect anyone, including you. Let's buy out of this trouble with a little neighborliness."

"But I'm on Ballew's side!" Mike said hotly. "If the Weybrights are in trouble, it's because they're a pack of crooks. Let them get out of their own mess."

Kate took the two plates to the stove, dished out the food and returned to the table. Her father rose, unsummoned, and sat down.

"All right, Dad," Kate went on, "if you won't do that then promise me one thing."

"I'll promise nothing till I hear what you're asking," Keefer said stubbornly.

"I don't know what the Weybrights will do to Ballew, but I know Lynch and Tucker won't take this lying down. If they start after Ballew, he'll beg for help." She paused. "From you and from Sam, the only two people who sympathize with him. I want you to promise you won't help him."

"Did you ask Sam that and did he promise?" her father asked slyly.

"He refused."

"Then so do I, Katie," Keefer said affably, and he began to eat.

The three Weybrights ate with the crew in the cook shack and at this morning's breakfast were eight of the ten men employed by Circle W. The other two were at a line camp and were due in today.

The overhead kerosene lamp was losing its fight against coming daylight and there was little talk among the crew except when food was wanted. Old Lynch sat at the head of the table with a son on either side of him and now Lee, looking down the table, wondered if these Circle W hands had heard of Ballew's piece in the *San Dimas Times*. Chances were they hadn't. Only a few of them could read and most of them had been riding all day, so were out of contact with gossip. The Spanish cook circled the table with the big granite coffeepot and now Lee crooked a finger at him. While his cup was being filled, he took out a sack of tobacco and rolled a smoke.

Under lowered lids, Lee watched his father finish breakfast and as he did so he wondered why there was no trace of anger in the old man's face. Tucker, he noticed, didn't bother to hide his savage mood and he wondered that the crew hadn't noticed it. Maybe they had and were pretending they hadn't.

Old Lynch fired up a cigar and now the hands, their hunger satisfied, started to talk among themselves as they rose from the table.

Suddenly, Lynch called out, "Wait a minute, boys." When the talk subsided and he had the attention of the crew, he said, "I've got some news. I want you to hear it. Let's go in the bunkhouse and let Fred clean up." He rose and went through the door behind his chair that led into the long bunkhouse which held the smell of unaired blankets and unwashed clothes. Tucker followed him and

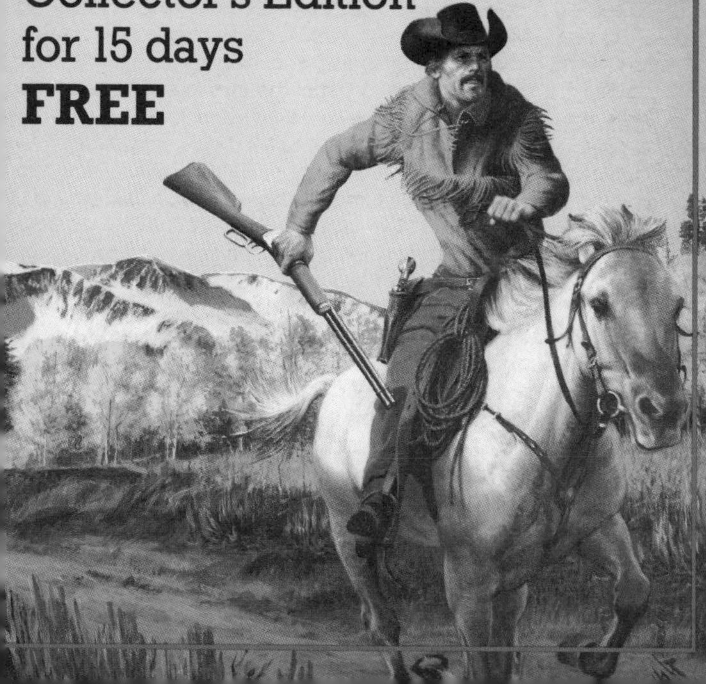

FLINT
IF HE HAD TO DIE, AT LEAST IT WOULD BE ON HIS TERMS...

Get a taste of the *true* West, beginning with the tale of *FLINT* FREE for 15 Days

Hunted by a relentless hired gun in the lava fields of New Mexico, Flint "*settled down to a duel of wits that might last for weeks...Surprisingly, he found himself filled with zest for the coming trial...So began the strange duel that was to end in the death of one man, perhaps two.*"

If gripping frontier adventures capture your imagination, welcome to The Louis L'Amour Collection! It's a handsome, hardcover series of thrilling sagas by the world's foremost Western authority and author.

Each novel in The Collection is a true-to-life portrait of the Old West, depicted with gritty realism and striking detail. Each is enduringly bound in rich, Sierra-brown leatherette, with padded covers and gold-embossed titles. And each may be examined and enjoyed for 15 days. FREE. You are never under any obligation; so mail the card at right today.

Now in handsome Heritage Editions

Each matching 6" x 9" volume in The Collection is bound in rich Sierra-brown leatherette, with padded covers and embossed gold title... creating an enduring family library of distinction.

Lee dropped in behind Tucker. The crew, he noticed, was quiet. Normally, Tucker dealt out work assignments at the corral and he knew these men were thinking that something special was slated for them.

Some of the men sat on their bunks and others stood around the gear-cluttered table in the center of the room.

When they were quiet, Lynch pulled a folded copy of the *San Dimas Times* from his pocket, opened it and without preliminary said, "Here's an advertisement that's printed in this week's *Times.*"

Lynch read it to them and when he was finished he looked around the room and saw that some of the simpler minds had not understood it, for a couple of the men were frowning in wonder. He said, "What this Ballew is saying is that he claims to own a good chunk of Circle W, that we're trespassing, and that anybody with a horse is invited to rustle our stock to clear the range he claims."

The crew exchanged glances and Lynch went on. "I don't know who'll be the first to accept his invitation, but we'll be ready for them. I've already sent a message to the Stoughtons and they'll throw in their crew with us."

Old Lynch dragged on his cigar before he continued. "It's impossible for us to ride boundary all the time from now on, so we'll have to do the next best thing." He paused. "Today I want you to push all our stuff back from the Breaks, push it east. I want you to travel in pairs. After we get our stuff pushed back I'll want the edge of the Breaks patrolled. If you see that any beef has been pushed into the Breaks, one of you stay with the tracks and the other bring back word to Bib S. We'll have help there for the tracker. I don't want the tracker to push things. All I want is for him to trail the beef until help comes. I can promise you this won't go on for very long."

"How can you promise, Dad?" Lee asked soberly.

Tucker cut in angrily, mad at nothing special, but mostly at the situation. "Because Ballew will be gone," Tucker said flatly.

Old Lynch spoke as if he hadn't heard Tucker, "Lee, you, Perez, and Billy are to disregard the orders I've given the rest." He paused as if to isolate this. "You're to hunt down Ballew and bring him in if you can. If you can't, leave him where he falls."

Tucker's face showed a new anger now, Lee saw. "Trade me for Lee, Dad," Tucker said.

Old Lynch shook his head. "Lee's got to learn sometime how we do this." His glance shifted to Perez, a wiry, grizzled Apache half-breed who was watching Lynch with a kind of sleepy alertness in his dark eyes.

"Lee," Lynch went on, "Perez is tracker. No arguments with his decision." Now he looked at Perez. "I want you to push Ballew, Perez. Don't let him sleep and don't let him eat. When you need fresh horses send Lee or Billy back here for them. You should have him in short order because I don't think he'll run. If he does, follow him."

Now his glance shifted to Billy Hudson, a young, square-faced, redheaded rider with a look of almost joyful belligerence in his face. "Billy, don't crowd it. I want him alive if possible." Now to all three men he said, "Better get going. Ballew left Dry Wells in mid-afternoon yesterday heading northwest. Pick up his trail there." He looked around him. "That's all."

Now the men headed for the corrals to pair off for the day's ride. The Weybrights stepped out into the new daylight. Tucker made his last try. "Dad," he began earnestly, "I wish you'd trade me and Lee. I've got a little score of my own to settle with Ballew."

Lynch shook his head. "No, I'll need you here, Tuck. This business of finding Ballew is important enough but what's more important is that we don't let ourselves be rustled blind. It's your job to stop that."

Tucker shrugged, said quietly to Lee, "Watch it, kid," and headed for the corral.

Lee looked at his father now and his expression was one of puzzlement. "Dad, you didn't make it very clear in there. Just what do you want us to do?"

Lynch looked at him in quiet astonishment and said, "I couldn't make it any clearer. I want you to get him and bring him in, preferably alive."

"Then what happens?"

Lynch hesitated. "I don't know any law and I'll leave that to Parry," Lynch said grimly. "Still, it would seem to me a man is inviting a jail sentence if he urges a mob of people to rustle another man's stock. His claim to this land is no good, which makes his piece in the paper a lie. It's like saying 'let's you and him fight'."

"But what if he doesn't want to come with us?" Lee persisted.

Old Lynch answered grimly, "It's up to you to make him come. I'm sure Perez knows some ways. I think Billy does too."

Lee knew he was dismissed, and he turned and tramped toward the horse corral. In spite of himself he couldn't help but feel the excitement. This was his first manhunt. He could shoot at a man and be shot back at. Privately he knew that his father wanted Ballew out of the way and he didn't care how this was achieved. He knew that Perez and Billy Hudson understood this too. It was strange, he thought, that a man could say one thing, mean another, and still have the meaning thoroughly understood by the men listening to him.

The hands, in pairs, were heading out for the Stoughtons' where they would be joined by the Bib S crew on the sweep along the edge of the Breaks.

Perez and Billy had already roped their mounts and were saddling. Lee took a look at the horses in his string and guessed that since this would probably be a long and grueling ride, he would sacrifice speed for durability in his mount. He singled out the big-chested bay, roped him, then moved over to his blanket and saddle which Perez had brought out with his own and put atop the corral pole.

As Lee was saddling, Billy Hudson said, "How'd your dad know Ballew was in Dry Wells yesterday?"

"A fellow came up to the house late last night and told him," Lee said.

"You reckon he'll throw in with one of those Breaks outfits?"

"Your guess is as good as mine," Lee said. He was surprised at the weariness in his voice.

"What's the difference?" Perez asked from the other side of his horse.

"Plenty," Billy said. "Are we going for one man or are we going to have to take him away from ten others?"

Now Perez straightened up and looked over his saddle. "Every man has got to be alone sometime," he said flatly. "That's the time we'll be there."

They mounted and set off in the southwesterly direction heading for the dug road that this part of the basin used to reach Dry Wells. It would be a good six-hour ride, Lee knew, and as they crossed this corner of Circle W range onto the Bib S, he wished that his father had elected Tucker in his place. It wasn't that he was scared; it was that he had no stomach for hunting a man, knowing what the end would be. He had seen dead men before, but this was the first time he had been told to help make one dead.

It was past the middle of a windy morning when they picked up the dug road at the edge of the Breaks. It dropped down through the dunes and could scarcely be called a road. Dug out long ago by the optimistic dry farmers who hoped to find a market for their produce in the basin, it had washed and eroded through neglect until it was little more than a track. Perez, because he had been appointed leader by old Lynch, put his horse onto the dug road first.

Lee, being the greenest and youngest, brought up the rear. Now that they were sheltered from the ground breeze off the flats, the morning grew hot. Since they were riding single file and conversation was difficult, they lapsed into silence by unspoken agreement. They were a half-hour deep into the Breaks when they came to a large clay dune which the dug road skirted halfway up its side. The track turned so abruptly around the dune that Lee almost lost sight of Perez. Then, abruptly, Perez reined in and raised his hand to halt them. Hudson pulled alongside Perez and Lee moved his horse up, although there was not enough room for the three of them abreast.

Perez immediately pointed to fresh tracks in the trail

and even Lee could see that here a rider coming their way had reined up and turned back.

Now Perez slowly turned his head and looked up the side of the dune. Hudson and Lee both followed his glance. There, squatting on his heels, gun hanging limp in his hand, was Giff Ballew.

"I wondered when you'd think to look about you," Ballew said drily. He rose, his gun arm slack along his leg.

Lee felt a faint chill touch his spine and he looked at the impassive Perez whose expression was bland and unreadable.

"Looking for me?" Giff asked.

Slowly Billy Hudson turned in the saddle to give Lee a warning glance, then he shifted his attention to Ballew.

"We're three," Billy Hudson said, a jeer in his voice. "If we make it a fight, you'll only get one of us before the others cut you down."

Giff raised his gun and shot at Huson. The slug caught Billy in the shoulder and knocked him out of the saddle and into Perez before he fell to the ground with a moaning grunt. With plain shock Lee looked at Ballew who, gun waist-high and pointed at them, stood utterly motionless.

"He was a fool to say that," Ballew said thinly. "You two want to make a fight of it?"

Hudson groaned and started to curse with pain.

"Do you?" Ballew pushed.

"No," Perez said quietly.

"Then you better get him back to your place," Ballew said. "Load him up."

Perez said, "Lee," and the youth dismounted. Perez tramped over to Hudson's horse, backed him away from the prone man, then knelt beside Hudson. When he rolled him over he saw that blood already pooled the dust. Hudson, white-faced and with closed eyes, was tugging at the neckerchief around his throat to stanch the blood.

Lee took off his own and Hudson's neckerchiefs,

opened the shirt and pressed both against the wound.
"Can you hold it there, Billy?" he asked.

Hudson nodded.

"First give me your good hand. You've got to get on
your feet."

Lee took Hudson's hand, ducked under his arm and
then heaved the wounded man to his feet. Perez led
Hudson's horse up and then reached over the saddle to
give Hudson a pull up.

With a shuddering groan of anguish, Hudson was
hoisted and pulled into his saddle. Lee turned his horse
around, and both he and Perez looked up at Ballew.

"Don't bother hunting me from now on," Ballew said
slowly, flatly. "I'll be hunting you."

Chapter Four

TUCKER WEYBRIGHT drew an old hand, Tim Carl, for a partner that morning, and when they reached the Bib S and saw that Stoughton's crew had already ridden out they did not bother to stop. Moving across the flats toward the Breaks they met two small herds of mixed Bib S and Circle W beef that were being pushed away from the Breaks by Rib S hands.

This was nothing but an imposed roundup of the two ranches, Tucker thought grimly. Here were two crews dedicating themselves to an act of cowardice. They were running from a threat carried on a piece of paper. It was as he told his father last night, the Breaks riffraff, without so much as a move, were depriving both ranches of a good chunk of their range. Nobody had raised a hand against them, but they were already on the run.

Lynch's judgment had prevailed, however. Where Tucker had wanted to ride into Dry Wells with a big crew which would give a show of force to his ultimatum, his father had insisted that their first duty was to save

their stock rather than scrap with phantom enemies. In
fact, Tucker thought privately, the only sensible thing
the old man had done was put in motion the hunt for
Ballew.

During most of the day he and Tim Carl accepted
and herded east the beef that the two crews were scour-
ing out along the edge of the Breaks. They would push
them a few miles eastward away from the Breaks and
then return for more. During that day Tucker's temper
did not improve. This act of humiliation was almost
physically embarrassing to him; he could almost see men
from the two-bit outfits around Dry Wells hiding in the
Breaks, watching and laughing.

Toward midday across the flats they could see that
the Bib S chuck wagon had been set up and they, along
with other passing riders, stopped for coffee and steak
sandwiches.

It was almost dark before Tucker, who had not exchanged a dozen words with the gray-haired and taciturn
Tim Carl, rode up and reined in.

"Better head back, Tim. We can finish this tomorrow." He regarded the older man with a kind of hot
speculation in his eyes as he shoved back his hat, folded
his arms and let his feet dangle free of the stirrup.
"Suppose you wanted to rustle yourself some beef tonight and had a place to hide them, where would you
start?"

Tim thought a moment, then said, "I sure wouldn't
start behind us. I'd have to ride five-seven miles before
I found anything."

"Then up ahead where we haven't reached yet. Is
that it?"

Tim nodded.

"Any special place?" Tucker prodded.

Again Tim reflected. "I'd figure I'd find a jag of stuff
that would come in for water into Soda Springs. That's
close to the Breaks and the springs' runoff from storms
has cut a pretty straight canyon down into the Breaks.
If they could be hazed into that canyon, there'd be no
place for them to go except deeper into the Breaks."
He shook his head and smiled faintly. "What I'd do

when I had them there I don't know. Sit down and eat them, maybe."

"Let's have your rifle," Tucker said irrelevantly.

Without a word Tim lifted his carbine from its boot and handed it to Tucker. "Tell Dad I'm going to stake myself out tonight. I got a feeling."

"Want any help?"

Tucker shook his head. "There'll be a moon later. That's all the help I'll need." He reined his horse around and rode off to the southeast while Tim, after watching him for a moment, pulled his pony around and headed back for Circle W.

Tucker arrived at Soda Springs an hour after dark. A few cattle spooked away as he moved his horse through the mud and into the small flat pond that held a strange-tasting but palatable water. After letting his horse drink its fill, he moved down parallel to the dry runoff trench until the grade began to pitch into the Breaks. Picketing his horse well to the east, Tucker returned to the canyon mouth and scouted his position. He picked his spot where anything going up or down the canyon would be between him and the coming moon. Then he settled himself in the sage that clung to the side of the canyon. Before rolling and carefully lighting a cigarette, he had tested the wind to make sure the updraft from the canyon would take his smoke onto the flats.

The peacefulness of the night was lost on Tucker and he could not have relaxed if he had wanted to. He listened without really concentrating and inevitably the happenings of the past few days that had so bitterly galled him marched in review. First and foremost was the beating he had received at Ballew's hands. Tucker blamed that on the treachery of surprise. He would welcome a bare-knuckle fight with Ballew and was sure he could win. When Circle W finally captured Ballew he would prove it. Next was the damned gall of the man. Even the thought of Ballew's piece in the *Times* had the power to enrage him.

He wondered then why Ballew had ridden over to Dry Wells. Was it to encourage the Wallings, the Bufords, the Olmsteds, and the Moores to raid Circle W,

or even to recruit them? He wondered, too, if Ballew
had seen and talked with Hannah. He couldn't very
well help it in that tiny spot, Tucker reflected wryly.
Would Hannah help him? Thinking carefully, Tucker
couldn't really answer that. Hannah was his woman,
there was no doubt about it, but when it came to pro-
tecting her kind and covering up for them, Tucker
simply couldn't reach her. Beatings, threats, and bribes
were of no avail. He knew that many times in the past a
tip from Hannah, even a hint of what was being planned
against Circle W and Bib S, would have saved hours of
riding and would have led to evidence that would have
jailed a man. Hannah would grant him any favor but
betrayal of her own kind, and he kept her at Kelsey's
as punishment. The day she spoke openly of what she
knew the Breaks outfits planned against Circle W, he
would move her to town or anywhere she wanted and
provide for her. Until then she could work as kitchen
help for the stage station.

Light on the horizon presaged the moon's rise and
presently Tucker saw it begin its climb into the sky. A
distant coyote saluted it and a couple of its pups took
up the chorus in treble. Tucker craved another cigarette, but wisdom dictated abstinence. In the increasing
light of the moon he could pick out the scattered cattle around the springs. He was watching them idly when
he was suddenly aware that one by one they were coming
to their feet. Had the coyotes moved in to have a look
at the new calves? Tucker doubted it. Their cries had
come from too far away.

Patiently he watched, trying to read a pattern into
this. Soon the cattle on the far side of the springs began
to move toward him, and then Tucker made out a dim
and uncertain form beyond these cattle. The rest of the
bedded cattle were heaving to their feet, but Tucker
was watching a shape he could not identify. Suddenly
a distant shrill whistle, the kind that some riders used
to chouse cattle ahead of them, came to him, and Tucker
felt his heart pound. The form he could not identify at
this distance had to be a rider carefully gathering in
those cattle around the springs.

Tentatively Tucker raised his rifle and sighted at a clump of sage skylined across the canyon. As he had hoped, the moonlight allowed him to see down the barrel of his carbine and, most important, to see the front sight. Turning his attention now to the cattle slowly moving toward the canyon mouth, he picked up the muffled "Hi—ya" of a man's voice that rode over the shrill whistle. There were two of them then, Tucker knew. Quietly he levered a shell into the carbine and swiftly considered if any light-colored article of clothing might give away his position. He would be in full moonlight on the side hill among the sagebrush. His shirt was a light-colored calico, his jacket of brown duck. Now he buttoned his jacket collar to hide the shirt, and because his hat was a little lighter than an earth color, he removed it and put it beside him. Sitting, he could use arm on knee to steady his shooting. Tucker waited.

The cattle, moving reluctantly, were approaching the canyon mouth and some of their calves were bawling. Now Tucker could pick out a rider on either side of the herd which numbered perhaps forty head, counting calves.

When the lead animal encountered the brush-choked canyon mouth, he veered off, but the swing rider on the far side hazed him back into the brush. With the other cattle piling up behind him, he plunged through the sage and was headed down the canyon, the others following. Tucker, however, had no eyes for the cattle; they could be retrieved tomorrow. It was the two men he was watching. Now that the herd was headed down the canyon the two riders reined in and then, when the last of the cattle had passed, they dropped in together at the rear.

The herd went slashing through the sage, passed below him and now Tucker lifted his rifle. At the canyon mouth the farthest rider, observing this was a single-file proposition, put his horse through the brush into the canyon. Following him with a rifle, sighting on him, Tucker saw with irritation that with the man's dark clothes, blending with the opposite canyon wall, he was difficult to see. The second rider was wearing a lighter shirt, and now experimentally Tucker sighted at him. He almost grunted with satisfaction when he saw that the lighter background picked up his sight clearly. Again he waited for perhaps five seconds until the first rider had passed below him. Then he drew in a deep breath, steadied his elbow on his knee, picked up the shirt of the second rider, followed him for a full second and then gently squeezed the trigger.

He heard his bullet slap home, heard the braying grunt of a man hit as the shot echoed loudly.

Momentarily blinded by the gun flash, Tucker nevertheless swung his gun trying to pick up the first rider. But even as he did so he heard the pounding hoofbeats of a suddenly spurred horse and heard a new and more urgent crashing of brush. A movement that was far up on the hillside attracted his attention and he sent a shot in that direction. There was no answer, but on the heels of his shot was the sound of a horse stampeding down the canyon.

Swiftly Tucker moved to the right, knowing that his two shots would pinpoint his location. For a full minute he made no attempt to go down into the canyon, but only listened to the receding racket of the cattle.

Presently, when the night was quiet again, he rose and moved slowly down into the shallow canyon. Almost on its brush-clogged floor he picked up the lighter color of the rider's shirt, and now he moved slowly, covering the figure with his rifle. In seconds he came to the figure of a man sprawled on his face in the sage. Tucker knelt beside him and rolled the lifeless body onto its back. His hand came away sticky and he ground it into the dirt before he reached in his jacket pocket for a match.

Wiping the match alight on his boot sole he held it up and looked into the open, staring and sightless eyes of Faye Olmsted. His shot, he saw, had caught Olmsted in the side at about the fourth rib. He had been dead, Tucker judged, before he hit the ground.

Rising now, Tucker felt a pleasant warmth come over him. He had killed the first man to accept Ballew's invitation. He leaned his carbine against the tall sage, fashioned a cigarette, lighted it, then listened. He doubted that the second man would return to this ambush. Chances were he was riding hell for leather for the safety of the Breaks.

Now Tucker considered the fate of Faye Olmsted. Humiliated at being caught rustling and set afoot, he had probably been only too eager to join someone else in the raid on Circle W beef. What to do with him? Tucker thought. Should he take the body into Dry Wells tonight and dump him on Kelsey's doorstep as a warning? No, it was too far to Dry Wells to pack a dead man. Should he leave him here with Ballew's advertisement in his hand as a warning to others? That, Tucker knew, would be foolish. Nobody would return for Olmsted's body. But Ballew must know that he had been the direct cause of Olmsted's death.

Slowly, almost painfully, the feeling came to Tucker that Ballew could and should be involved in Olmsted's death. He was at Dry Wells yesterday, wasn't he? There was no proof that he hadn't put Faye Olmsted up to this. As far as that went, there was no proof that the second man wasn't Ballew. Could it be made to look as if Ballew and Olmsted were in this together?

Then, with a shock of recollection, Tucker remembered his fight with Ballew. He had almost strangled Ballew by twisting the neckerchief around his throat and probably could have if the neckerchief hadn't torn. The yellow neckerchief he remembered all too well, because the sight of it reminded him of his defeat; it was lying alongside the road beyond Circle W.

What if this neckerchief could be found in Faye Olmsted's hand? Couldn't it be made to look as if Ballew and Olmsted had quarreled, fought, and Ballew had killed him? That would put the whole country on Ballew.

Tucker threw down his cigarette, ground it out, and then remembering, picked up the butt and put it in his pocket. He had some riding to do tonight, he thought with grim satisfaction, but it would be worth it. Ballew's yellow cavalry neckerchief was an oddity in this country and would be remembered by a dozen people. It was strange that rustling partners should quarrel in the middle of the act of rustling, but that was something Sheriff Corbett would have to figure out.

Tucker, happier than he had been for days, picked up his rifle and headed for his picketed horse and the long ride for the yellow neckerchief.

From his vantage point that morning at the edge of the Breaks, it did not take Giff long to figure out what Circle W and Bib S crews were out to do. It was obvious they were pushing both spread's cattle to the east where it would be more difficult for the Breaks outfits to drive them off. As Giff watched a distant pair of riders hazing a small bunch of cattle east, he remembered that he had seen five such small herds being pushed in the same direction this very morning.

Kneeling on one knee to rest his saddle-weary legs, Giff fumbled in his shirt pocket for the last of his cigars. Shifting the reins to his other hand, he struck a match with his fingernail, fired up his cigar and considered his situation. There was little doubt in his mind that he was being trailed. After yesterday's meeting with Lee Weybright and the two Circle W hands, he knew that he had perhaps bought a little time. Either Lee or the other hand, but not necessarily both, would have had to return with the wounded man to Circle W. On the assumption that they would try to trick him into believing that all three would return to the ranch, Giff had spent most of yesterday crossing the Breaks in a southerly direction. He had kept moving and he had been careful to seek out terrain where tracking would be difficult and time-wasting. Last night he had slept close to a spring whose overflow watered a patch of wild hay that provided grazing for his weary horse. At first daylight he was up and moving, assuming again that he was being trailed and anxious to keep ahead of his pursuers.

Now as he watched the small band of cattle growing smaller as they moved across the flats, an idea came to him. Instead of remaining a virtual prisoner of the Breaks here was an opportunity to dash out, confuse and lose whoever was trailing him. Why not ride out boldly onto the flats, pick up a half-dozen head of cattle and push them east just as the two ranch crews were doing? At a distance it would appear to an observer that he was just another Circle W hand on his lone business.

He wiped the coal off the tip of his cigar, put the stub in his pocket and then stepped into the saddle. Moving along the edge of the Breaks, he soon saw a scattered group of cattle, and he moved out toward them. It was the work of only a few minutes to round up the small band and push them east. In the distance to the north of him he saw a lone rider moving a bunch even smaller than his own. In the next half hour Giff noticed that this rider was trying to join him and throw the two bands together. Giff, however, kept drifting a little south, keeping the original distance between himself and the other rider. Presently, the rider gave up this effort to join the two herds and veered straight east.

Giff kept watching his back trail and he could see no indication that he was being followed. A pair of riders heading south passed far ahead of him, paying him no attention. And now Giff considered his immediate future. It was too soon to tell if his advertisement in the *Times* had the desired effect. One thing for certain, it had alerted both these big ranches to the potential danger of large-scale rustling. It had also set them on him. After yesterday's shooting, he guessed the Weybrights would take an even grimmer view of his presence in this country. Once the two crews had pushed their beef into relative safety, they would concentrate on hunting him down. Well, if his plans for today worked, they would have a lot of country to cover.

When Giff spotted an abandoned band of cattle to the north, he knew that this was as far as the two crews were pushing the cattle, and now he abandoned his own bunch and cut north. When he approached these bands, he put his horse angling through them, knowing that in their grazing they would obliterate his tracks. Constantly watching his back trail, he spent a good bit of that day riding through the scattered bands of grazing cattle until he was sure sometime in the afternoon that no pursuer could possibly have followed his trail through deep grass, across rocky flats, and across dry hard pan that cattle would cross after him.

He turned now to the problem of immediate importance. His grub was running low and he must replenish it. He calculated that he could risk one more furtive visit to either Harmony or Dry Wells, since both ranch crews were still busy moving their stuff away from the Breaks. The thought of Harmony reminded him of Sam Furman and Kate Miles. He wondered if Lynch Weybright had vented his anger on the paper and he guessed the old boy would have been too busy with other affairs. Besides, with Kate Miles present Giff doubted if Lynch would resort to violence. He wondered then if he would ever see Kate Miles in anything but an angry mood. Only the first few minutes of their first meeting had held any friendliness. The times they had seen each other afterward, she was sharp, unfriendly, often angry, and always resentful of his presence. That was her privilege he conceded, since her philosophy of peace at any price—the price to be paid by himself—seemed precious above all things to her.

But before he rode farther there was a promise he had to keep, he remembered. And now, in the dusk, he swung in an arc to the west where he judged the Circle W lay on its timbered mesa.

It was dark when he picked up the lights of Circle W. He crossed the road and put his horse deep in the timber, then dismounted and tied it. Moving toward the ranch buildings, he halted at the edge of the timber, recalling the layout. He tried to remember if, on his other visit, there had been any dogs about, and he could recall none. He supposed that the crew would work until dark and with the long ride from the Breaks would be drifting in late. He must keep this in mind, he knew.

Now he started for the house, pausing often to listen and to watch. Presently, he began his circle so that the corral would be between him and the bunkhouse. There was a lantern hanging from the corral gate. Even as he approached, a pair of riders came in from the west, unsaddled, turned their horses into the corral and van-

ished in the direction of the bunkhouse. Giff allowed
a couple of minutes for them to reach the cook shack,
then he moved up to the corral, circled it and the barn
and headed for the bunkhouse-cook shack. He noted that
there was no lamp lighted in the main house.

Now he approached the bunkhouse, and he was both
silent and cautious. Achieving its log wall, he moved
toward a window and carefully peered inside. A pair of
Circle W hands were playing cards at the big table and
he could see the back of one man lying in his bunk, back
to the overhead light.

Then he moved on along the wall toward the cook
shack and the end of the building and again cautiously
edged up so he could look through the window. There
were four men at the table, one of them Lynch Weybright who was smoking a cigar. Neither Lee Weybright
nor the dark Indian-looking hand with him yesterday were at the table. Giff backed off into the night,
circled the barn and halted in its shadow where he could
observe the corral. It was Lee Weybright that he must
see and apparently Lee had not come in yet.

Patiently he waited in the darkness while another pair
of riders rode up, off-saddled, turned their horses into
the corral and moved on toward the cook shack. By another hour he was about ready to gve up when he heard
the sound of approaching horses. Peering through the
corral poles he saw by the light of the lantern the corral
gate open. Lee Weybright and the Indian-looking man
rode their horses into the corral and dismounted. Had
they been hunting him today? he wondered .

Now, drawing his gun and bent over, he moved along
the upright poles of the corral until he reached the
gate. Then he straightened and moved into the lantern light. Both men had their backs to him. Giff put
a foot on the lower bar of the gate, folded his arms on
top of it, his gun trailing from his right hand. It was
the Indian who first lifted the saddle, then his saddle
blanket from his mount and turned. He saw Giff immediately and abruptly halted. He opened his mouth
as if to speak and then closed it, watching Giff.

Now Lee lifted his saddle from his horse, pulled off the saddle blanket and turned. He, too, saw Giff immediately.

"Why don't you quit hunting me?" Giff asked drily. "I told you I'd hunt you."

Neither of the men answered; they watched him warily, and Lee's face was stiff with anger.

"Have I got to shoot you?" Giff asked mildly.

Again neither of them answered.

Giff decided to take a chance and said, "You were both hunting me today." It was not a question, but a statement, and he saw Lee Weybright nod.

"Keep it up and you're dead," Giff said. "You could be dead now." He paused. "Want to yell for help?"

The Indian said nothing, but Lee cleared his throat and said, "No," adding quietly, "damn you."

"Why, I'll call help for you," Giff jeered. "Let's see who I can turn out." Almost casually he raised his gun, aimed at the lantern and shot.

As the light was wiped out, Giff moved, but not in the direction from which he had come. He passed the gate and was again behind the corral poles, and now he moved swiftly and quietly along them. He was reasonably certain that neither the Indian nor Lee would go for their guns. Their position was pinpointed and they had no way of knowing if his gun wasn't aimed at one of them.

Quietly he moved out into the darkness and was heading for his horse when he heard a call from the bunkhouse, "Who's there? Sing out!"

"Ballew's here!" It was the Indian who yelled.

Giff halted long enough to see the first two men boil through the bunkhouse doorway, then he turned and headed for the timber. They would be afraid to hunt him by lantern light, he knew, and in no special hurry, he found his horse, mounted, and headed out.

Kate Miles and Sam Furman were doing shop work this morning, and Kate had been in the front office a half-dozen times already to fetch things. This time when she entered and started across the room she halted abruptly. Old Lynch Weybright, ramrod-straight, was seated in the chair behind Sam's desk.

"I'm sorry. I didn't hear you come in," Kate said.

Weybright tipped his head. "I'd like to talk with your boss."

Kate felt the old fear start and she knew with dismal certainty that Sam's gun was in the right-hand drawer of the desk at which Weybright was seated.

"He just stepped across the alley. I'll go fetch him."

Kate went back into the shop and approached Sam, who was quietly tinkering with the job press. She touched him and when he looked up, she put her finger to her lips and beckoned him, then started for the back door.

Rising, a look of puzzlement on his face, Sam followed her. Kate opened the door, stepped into the alley and Sam came out, shutting the door behind him. "What's all this?"

"Lynch Weybright's in the front, looking for you. Your gun's in the right-hand drawer and he's sitting at the desk." She hesitated, then tilted her head in the direction of the back door to the store across the alley. "Can't you borrow one from the saddle shop?"

Sam took a deep breath, crossed the alley and went into the back door of Mitchell's Saddle Shop. He appeared in a moment with a gun rammed in his waistband and without a word to Kate stepped through the rear door of the shop. Kate followed him and she resolved that she would butt in on this conference even if Weybright or Sam asked her to leave. She knew the two men were far less likely to fight if she were present.

Sam stepped through the office door and Kate behind him said, with a bright obviousness, "Here he is, Mr. Weybright."

Old Lynch silently regarded Sam, noting the gun jutting out from behind the inkstained apron. Now Lynch reached up to the breast pocket of his buttonless vest and drew out the two halves of a torn yellow neckerchief. Placing them on the desk, he asked quietly, "Ever seen this before?"

Sam walked up to the desk and picked up one half

of the neckerchief, examined it and then said, "Should I have?"

Lynch's glance shuttled to Kate. "Have you, Mrs. Miles?"

Now Kate came up to the desk too. She could remember well enough and, although she had no notion of what Lynch Weybright was driving at she saw no reason to lie. "It's Giff Ballew's, isn't it?"

Weybright's glance shuttled back to Sam. "Is it, Furman?"

"I don't know," Sam said slowly. "He was wearing one like it the first day I saw him."

"Outside of a yellowleg, have you seen anyone else wear one like it?"

Sam shook his head in negation. Weybright picked up the two pieces of the neckerchief, folded them and tucked them back into his vest pocket. "I'm on my way to Sheriff Corbett to show it to him," Lynch said, and then paused as if to isolate what he was about to say. "It was found in the hands of a dead man. Not by me but by one of Overton's riders."

"What dead man?" Sam asked.

"Faye Olmsted, Harvey Olmsted's brother. Faye and another man were driving off some Circle W beef. Nobody knows why they fought where they did, but Olmsted's shirt was ripped off before he was shot."

Kate asked sharply, "Are you implying that the other man was Ballew?"

"Don't the facts speak for themselves?" Weybright countered.

"You think Ballew and Olmsted were rustling your stuff?" Sam asked.

"How do I know?" Lynch said coldly. "There were tracks of two horses. We found Olmsted at the head of the canyon and the beef down below it."

"He wouldn't do that," Sam said flatly.

"What? Rustle or kill?"

"Neither one."

"Would you say that he would stop three Circle W riders, among them my son, and shoot one for no cause?"

"He did that?" Kate asked.

"He did," Weybright said flatly. "In broad daylight. There was no mistaking him. My son Lee identified him and my son is no liar. The hurt man's in my bunkhouse with a bullet hole in his shoulder."

Neither Kate nor Sam spoke, and now Lynch came out of the chair to tower above him. Lynch went on: "You might say this is thanks to you, Furman."

"That advertisement?"

Lynch nodded.

"Why don't you go back a little and thank yourself," Sam said quietly. "If the deed book in the courthouse hadn't been tampered with, none of this would have happened."

Slowly Lynch pulled his gun from its holster, laid it on the desk and said, "I'm waiting for you to say I tampered with it."

"Be careful, Sam," Kate cut in.

But Sam Furman was angry, and it seemed to Kate that a kind of recklessness touched him.

"I can't say because I can't prove it, Weybright. I do know who would benefit, however, and so do you."

Weybright nodded, picked up his gun, holstered it, and said, "Don't take any more advertisements from Ballew, Furman. You'll print *nothing* you can't prove either."

"You bet I won't!" Furman said. "For instance, I can't prove that business with the neckerchief, and neither can you!"

"I can prove he shot Billy Hudson."

"There must have been a reason," Sam said flatly. "When I find the reason I'll print it."

"Then keep in touch with Sheriff Corbett," Weybright said flatly. He turned and tramped out of the room, closing the door behind him with a surprising gentleness.

Kate looked at Sam. "Do you believe what he said about Ballew?"

"About the rustling, no. About shooting one of Weybright's hands, I don't know. Maybe he was crowded into it."

Kate walked over to the chair behind the desk and

wearily sank into it. "Well, it's started." Her voice was dispirited. "I knew it would. Olmsted's murder will touch it off. The Circle W bunch will be sure that Ballew and Olmsted were rustling their beef. They'll pick on the Breaks bunch and they'll retaliate."

"My God, wouldn't you?" Sam asked.

Kate said bitterly, "Every Circle W and Bib S rider will turn up a deputy. The law will be what each one of them thinks it is."

"If you think that way, why don't you talk to the Weybrights?" Sam said angrily.

Kate said with bitterness, "Sure. Who'd be likely to listen to me? Tucker wouldn't listen to anybody and Lee does what the other two tell him. If there were only some womenfolk in that family that could make them listen to sense."

"There's Myra Stoughton," Sam said.

"She's just another Weybright with a dress on."

Sam grinned. "Well, there's always Tucker's girl at Dry Wells."

"Hannah Moore?"

Sam nodded.

"What business would I have going to her?"

"None, Katie," Sam's voice was almost sharp. "You've been trying to stop this ever since you saw Ballew. Let it happen. It's inevitable and you can't do anything about it. Why do you want to? The haves and the have-nots have always fought." He paused. "Besides, what have you got at stake in this row?"

"We'll all be forced to take sides eventually, Sam. I know what side my father will take. When he does, we're ruined."

Sam turned almost angrily. "Then keep on with your psalm singing and see where it gets you."

He strode back into the shop and Kate heard him slam the back door on his way to return the borrowed gun. Sam's reference to Hannah Moore as one of the Weybright womenfolk had been a joking one, Kate knew. Rumor had it that Hannah's child was Tucker's and that, with his usual arrogance, he had refused to make it legitimate. He kept Hannah at Dry Wells, visited her and openly flaunted their relationship. But did she have any influence on Tucker? A woman who couldn't influence a man to marry her probably couldn't influence him in other things. Besides, what could Hannah Moore say to that wild and arrogant Tucker that would change his ways? He had been baiting the poor ranchers for years, abusing them and accusing them, almost daring them to cross him.

Maybe Sam's joking reference made more sense than he knew. Maybe Hannah could stop this, since her family had been involved. At least it was worth a try.

She rose and went back into the shop where Sam had resumed his tinkering of the job press.

Halting beside him she said, "I'm taking the day off, Sam."

He looked up. "Now what? Megrims?"

"I'm going to take your advice and go see Hannah Moore."

Sam straightened up and looked at her with a kind of sadness in his eyes. "If you think you should do it, go ahead."

Kate nodded and went back into the office, put on her hat and stepped out into the street. At the livery stable she waited until her horse was hitched to the buggy and then drove out into the sunny morning on the Dry Wells road.

Now she had a chance to consider the information old Lynch had given them this morning. Ballew was surely a troublemaker, but she did not think he would throw in with a man of Faye Olmsted's type, quarrel with him and shoot him. Kate was certain that Ballew would disdain this method of revenging himself on Weybright. It was petty and ineffectual, not like him. She wished though that she had the details of his shooting a Circle W hand. There must have been some justification, if any shooting could ever be justified.

Sometime around midday the southbound stage passed her and afterward she was on the grade that let down into the Breaks. It had been a long time since she had been in this barren country, and observing it she could understand the bitterness of the families who had been forced to accept it.

The stage had already departed the Dry Wells station when she arrived. She left her horse and buggy under one of the big cottonwoods and regarded the long adobe building that housed the store and bar and the restaurant. She had forgotten how shabby the place was. It seemed exactly to fit the country and its people.

Passing the bar entrance Kate went to the door beyond which opened onto the dining room. It was empty and the table bare. She looked through the room into the kitchen which was also empty. Returning to the dining room, she heard voices in the bar and moved through the doorway into the adjoining room. A couple of men in the bar whom she did not know ceased their conversation and one-armed Kelsey, following their glances, turned his head.

"Where can I find Hannah, Mr. Kelsey?"

"Her house is out back. She's likely putting the baby to bed for a nap, Mrs. Miles."

Kate thanked him, withdrew into the restaurant, crossed the tidy kitchen and let herself out onto the hard-packed clay of the yard. A small adobe building lay to her right, and now she crossed the yard in the hot sun, halted in front of the door of the weather-eroded adobe and knocked on the doorframe. She heard a movement inside and then Hannah Moore appeared in the doorway, squinting against the sun.

When Hannah saw it was Kate Miles, surprise washed over her dark face. Then she said with her customary candor, "Why, Mrs. Miles, what are you doing out here?"

"I came to talk with you, Hannah. May I come in?"

Hannah nodded and stepped aside to let Kate enter the room. It was small and sparsely furnished, with a horsehair sofa, two chairs, a table against one wall and a lamp. Kate supposed the closed door in the opposite wall led into a bedroom where Hannah's child was napping.

Kate chose the sofa and Hannah Moore sat down in

ne of the chairs, placidly folding her hands in her lap.
he was a pretty girl, Kate thought, and at the moment
uspicious, probably justifiably so.

"Hannah, maybe I've come to you on a foolish
rrand," Kate began. "I hope you won't think it's
oolish, though."

Hannah only frowned and nodded that she under-
tood.

"You've probably heard of the advertisement in last
veek's *Times* that is causing so much trouble."

Hannah nodded.

"Did you know that Faye Olmsted was killed while
 e was rustling Circle W beef?"

"I heard it," Hannah said briefly.

"Did you also hear that Giff Ballew, who placed the
 d in the *Times*, shot and wounded a Circle W hand?"

"I hadn't, but good for him," Hannah said.

"What do you mean, 'good for him'?"

"If more Circle W hands were shot this would be a
 etter country."

Kate frowned. This was not going the way she had
 lanned it. "You sound as if you disliked Circle W."

"I hate everything about it," Hannah said flatly.

Kate said sharply, with a total lack of tact, "Including
 ucker Weybright?"

"I can't say that," Hannah said slowly. "Tucker is
 y child's father and I consider myself his wife, but I
 ate his family and all they stand for." She paused.
 Remember we were one of the families that Lynch
 unned off that range?"

"I remember it and I'm glad you do, too. I guess
 hat's why I'm here." Hannah scowled, but Kate went
 n. "Do you want to see those times come back?"

Hannah shook her head in negation, her face sad with
 he memory. "I lost two brothers. No, I don't want
 hose times back," Hannah said.

"They'll be back if we don't stop them," Kate said.

"They're almost here now." Hannah's voice was quiet.

"Isn't there something *you* can do?"

"Like what?"

"Haven't you any influence with Tucker? Can't you

make him see what's happening and what is going t
happen?" Hannah shrugged. "Unless somebody use
some sense, we'll be at one another's throats again.
was pretty small, but I can remember when there use
to be a funeral a day."

Hannah nodded. "Tucker would like those days back.
Her voice was bitter and almost angry.

"How do you mean?"

"Tucker hates all these families that Lynch chase
off Circle W. He'd like to chase them out of here too
He wants trouble. It will give him an excuse to gang u
on anyone he dislikes."

"But haven't you any influence with him?"

"He would beat me," Hannah said simply. "He—"
A knock on the doorframe interrupted her, an
Kelsey, his underwear seeming even dirtier in the brigh
sunlight, moved his head into the doorway. "Hannal
a man wants a meal. Can you fix it?"

"I'll be right in," Hannah said. She stood up an
Kate rose too. "It's no use trying, Mrs. Miles. I'm di
under his feet. He's glad about all that's happening. I
Ballew hadn't stirred it up, I think Tucker would have.
She shook her head. "I'm no help to you, none."

"I—I don't understand about you and Tucker."

"Hardly anybody does," Hannah said bitterly. "Ever
thing he does is wrong and I hate it, but he's my ma
and he gave me my child. Is that too hard to under
stand?"

"I guess not," Kate said quietly.

Kate moved to the door and stepped outside, Hannal
following. Together they walked toward the kitche
door. "If you're getting somebody a meal, would it b
too much trouble to fix me something to eat?" Kate sai
kindly.

"That's my job. Come in and sit down."

Kate stepped into the kitchen. "Can't I help you?"

"It won't take a minute. It's mostly ready. You g
in and rest yourself."

Kate went on into the empty dining room and sa
down. The word foolish did not begin to describe he

errand, she thought. She had assumed that Tucker Weybright, for all his faults, held some affection for the mother of his child and, holding that affection, it was reasonable to think Hannah could influence him. But Hannah's description of Tucker's relationship with her shocked and stunned Kate. Tucker Weybright was an animal, and out of some pathetic craving for love and affection, Hannah Moore still tolerated him.

Hannah came out of the kitchen, moved across the room to the bar doorway, halted and said to someone in the saloon, "Your dinner's ready."

Kate glanced up just in time to see Giff Ballew, unshaven and dusty, enter the room.

When Giff saw her he halted abruptly and stared at her in silence, a look of puzzlement on his face. Kate knew he was wondering what she was doing here and the thought brought a mild anger to her. If asked, she could say that she was trying to mend the harm that his stubbornness had done.

"I didn't think you ever got out this way," Ballew said, and he took off his hat and moved over to the bench opposite her and sat down.

"I hadn't figured on coming out until Lynch Weybright stopped by the shop this morning on his way to the sheriff's. You know what he wanted to show Sam and me?"

Giff shook his head, watching her.

"A yellow cavalry neckerchief that was found in the hand of a dead man, a man who had been shot."

"All right," Giff said in a puzzled voice.

"When I first laid eyes on you you were wearing a yellow cavalry neckerchief. Do you still have it?"

Giff looked beyond her and smiled at Hannah Moore as she entered. Hannah placed a plate of food before Kate, then rounded the table and set Giff's place before him. Wordlessly then she retired to the kitchen.

Kate saw Giff's glance raise to her. "Yes, I had a cavalry neckerchief. Tucker Weybright tried to choke me with it and it tore in two. The last I saw of it, it was lying in the brush along the road to Circle W."

Kate tried to determine if he was lying, but he wa
watching her carefully, no uneasiness in his deep-se
eyes and long face.

"Then how do you account for its being in Faye
Olmsted's hand when he was found dead?"

"I don't," Ballew said curtly, and he began to eat.

Kate put her attention to her dinner. She was hungry
and the food tasted good. Occasionally she would glance
at Ballew, trying to fathom his apparent indifference
to the news she had brought. Hannah Moore came in
with two cups and the coffeepot and poured them both
coffee before she retreated again into the kitchen.

When Ballew had drunk the last of his coffee he
reached in the pocket of his dusty shirt, brought out a
cigar and lighted it, then he turned his attention upon
her. "You haven't told me what that neckerchief ha
to do with your visit here."

Kate had the coffee cup halfway to her lips. She
halted it and set the cup down, feeling a rising irrita
tion. "Faye Olmsted was rustling Circle W beef when
he was killed. Lynch Weybright thinks that you and
Faye were there together, that you quarreled and fought
and that you killed him."

She saw Ballew's mocking smile that only kindled her
irritation. She went on, "I don't know or care who
killed Faye Olmsted. You could have killed him directly
or you could have killed him indirectly because he
believed your ad. The reason I'm here is to try and
stop this senseless fight before it really gets started. I
thought Hannah might have some influence on Tucker.'

"Not that kind of influence," Ballew said drily.

"I found that out." Kate's voice almost took on a
note of anger as she went on. "I found out something
else from Lynch Weybright. He said you shot one o
his crew. Is that true?"

"It is." Ballew's voice was flat, challenging.

"Maybe you can tell me why"

"I can *try* to tell you why," Ballew said, little pa
tience in his voice. "I surprised the three of them on
the road from Circle W to here. I had been tipped of
they would be hunting me and they admitted they were

One man took a look at me and started to tell the other two to go for their guns. He was suggesting that one of them was bound to kill me before I could get all three of them. I shot him. Quick!"

"Just for talking?" Kate asked.

Ballew nodded. "Just for talking. That talk would have got me dead. With him out of the way the other two were afraid to gang up on me."

"You make it sound pretty casual," Kate said.

"I didn't mean it to," Giff said drily. "It was anything but casual. It was think and act quickly or take their gunfire."

Kate drank the last of her coffee.

"Did you say Lynch stopped in at your shop on his way to the sheriff?" Ballew said.

Kate nodded.

Ballew grimaced wryly. "I've heard that Sheriff Corbett and Lynch Weybright understand each other."

"I think they'll understand each other so well that the sheriff will be looking for you."

"He'll have a lot of company," Giff said. "I—" His glance lifted beyond Kate's shoulder and Kate turned her head to see Hannah standing in the doorway.

"Tucker and a couple of his men just dismounted in front of my house," Hannah said.

Chapter Five

AS HE approached Dry Wells, Tucker caught sight of the horse and buggy under the cottonwoods and, curiosity prodding him, he kneed his horse in the direction of the buggy instead of riding up to the saloon tie rail where three saddle horses were already tethered. The two Circle W hands fell in beside him and the three of them reined in by the buggy.

"That's Mike Keefer's brand," one of the riders observed.

"It's Mrs. Miles," Tucker said. "I wonder what she's doing here?"

His glance lifted to the small adobe building where Hannah lived. He touched his horse and rode across the hard-packed clay and dismounted by the house. The two riders trailed him and reined up, waiting for orders.

Tucker stuck his head through the doorway and called, "Hannah." When he got no answer he wheeled and headed for the kitchen door. Halfway there Hannah came out and walked toward him.

Without preliminaries Tucker tipped his head toward the horse and buggy and said, "What's she doing out here?"

"Nothing that would interest you," Hannah said. "Come on in the house. I've got to get Lilly up from her nap."

"Let her go. Can you feed us?"

"All right. You can come through the kitchen." Hannah turned and started back for the kitchen door and now Tucker said to the two riders, "There's water at the corral. As soon as you're through with the horses come and eat."

He followed Hannah into the kitchen and noted a soiled cup and plate on the sink top. Hannah, with her back to him said, "I'll only be a minute."

Tucker stepped into the dining room and halted in the doorway. Kate Miles was seated alone in the dining room and, at Tucker's entrance, she turned. Meeting this wife of Dan Miles, the man he had killed, was never comfortable for Tucker. He had no regrets over the shooting and knew that he had been justified, but each time he saw her the thought came to him that he had widowed her and that she would hate him until she died. Touching his hat he said, "Queer place for you, Kate." He thought he smelled cigar smoke and supposed that it came from one of the bar patrons.

"I had an errand out this way and found myself hungry."

"For a stage station cook, Hannah's all right," Tucker conceded. He added, "I don't think a woman should be driving alone these days."

Kate's dark eyebrows lifted. "Why not?"

"All I can say is that I'm not riding alone any more."

"But I'm not *you*," Kate said quietly. "I've never even suspected anybody out this way of stealing our beef."

Tucker looked at her balefully, "Well, there's a killer loose."

"So your father told me."

"A lot of people from now on will be shooting first and explaining afterward."

"Isn't that what you want?"

"I don't mind it a bit," Tucker said grimly. "I just wouldn't want you in the middle."

"It's hard to mistake a woman in a buggy for a wanted killer. Maybe you're right though. I'll watch out."

Tucker nodded and walked into the bar. Kelsey was at the far end of the room, rearranging his sorry array of canned goods that Ballew had earlier depleted. A pair of strange riders were at the mahogany.

Kelsey turned at the sound of Tucker's entrance and a look of shock came into his broad face. Both the customers at the bar had their backs to him and Kelsey gestured with his good arm to the door. Then he came forward saying, "How are you, Tucker?" and stepped outside. In a moment Tucker, whose curiosity was aroused by Kelsey's actions, stepped outside.

Kelsey was waiting for him at the corner of the building. "Did you see him?" Kelsey asked.

"Who?"

"Ballew. He left a couple of minutes ago."

Wrath came to Tucker's dark face. "Why in hell didn't you call me?"

"I didn't know you were here! When'd you come in? Where's your horse?"

"Which way did he go?" Tucker demanded.

"I didn't pay any attention, Tuck. He bought some grub, asked for a meal, left his money on the bar and went out. I didn't even know you were around."

"All right, all right," Tucker said wearily. "I came in the back. I saw Mrs. Miles' buggy and went to ask Hannah what she was doing here." He scrubbed his face with his hand and cursed himself. Ballew could even have ridden out past the two hands watering the horses and they wouldn't have known him. He said roughly, "Go pour me some whiskey, Kelsey."

Back in the bar he poured himself a quick drink, downed it, and was pouring another when the two Circle

W riders came in. They also asked for whiskey. "See anybody ride out of here?" Tucker asked them.

One man shook his head, the other said, "Wasn't looking."

He had missed meeting Ballew by the merest fluke and that was what truly angered him. Eventually, of course, Ballew would be cornered, but he wanted to be the one to corner him. Ballew's visit to the Circle W last night was his warning to Perez and Lee. His shooting out the lantern in defiance of the whole crew was an intolerable thing. At the meeting between Lynch and his two sons at the house afterward, even Lynch was impressed by Ballew's daring. He had given his sons orders never to travel alone and this morning when he saw Sheriff Corbett he was going to tell him the same thing. Tucker had interrupted then and said grimly, "Tell Corbett not to bother hunting for Ballew, Ballew will come to him."

If what he planned for this afternoon was successful, perhaps Ballew wouldn't be having such an easy time. When he went back into the dining room Kate Miles was gone. Tucker went into the kitchen. Hannah was dishing up three plates of food. "You feed Ballew?" Tucker asked her.

Hannah looked directly at him. "Yes."

"Was he in the dining room when I rode in?"

"Yes."

"Then why didn't you tell me?" Tucker demanded angrily.

Hannah's answer was chill. "You know I won't tell you anything that goes on around here, Tucker. You can't make me."

"If I give the word Kelsey will fire you," Tucker said slowly. Both bafflement and anger were in his lean face.

"I know you could. If you did, your daughter would have a harder time eating, is all."

"Damn my daughter!" Tucker said angrily. He seemed undecided as to whether or not he was going to hit her, and then the sound of the two Circle W riders

pulling out a bench broke into his anger. He turned
and went into the dining room, and Hannah followed
with the food.

After they had eaten, Tucker and his two hands paid
up and left. Tucker did not bother to say hello to his
daughter or good-by to Hannah.

They rode northwest now in the direction of the
distant San Dimas range, and it was through dry hard
scrabble country that wouldn't graze one head to forty
acres. In midafternoon they left this seldom-traveled
road at a gate that sagged open, and ahead of them
a quarter mile they could see Olmsted's place. The
principal building was a log cabin with a sagging porch.
Rickety sheds adjoined the cedar-pole corral and in the
middle of the barn lot was a rusting grindstone. The
whole layout spoke of poverty, shiftlessness, and indifference, Tucker thought. It was a typical Breaks ranch,
except that there were no dirty kids underfoot.

Almost to the house Harvey Olmsted stepped through
the open door, a rifle cradled in his arm. He was a tall,
unshaven man of middle age, in tatterdemalion clothes
and split boots. He was hatless and his bald head was
an almost obscene white above his sun-browned and
dirty face.

"That's far enough!" he called out.

Tucker said to the Circle W riders, "Stay here," and
at his orders they reined up. Tucker continued on to
the porch and turned his horse so that when he dismounted Harvey Olmsted could see that he was not
going for his gun.

Slowly then Tucker turned, briefly looked over the
layout, grimaced, and then regarded Olmsted. "Put it
up, Harvey. I want to talk with you."

Hesitantly Olmsted came out onto the porch, then,
as if he knew the uselessness of any real opposition to
a Weybright, he leaned his gun against the wall and
came out to the steps. Watching him, contempt in his
eyes, Tucker was fairly certain that it was Harvey who
had sided Faye the night of the shooting. Lazily then,
Tucker sat down on the porch step and waited for

Harvey to sit down beside him. When Harvey did, he smelled; Tucker moved off a couple of feet.

"Corbett been out yet?" Tucker asked.

Harvey's bleached eyes regarded him with suspicion. "Why would he come here?"

"He will. And I think you'd better be ready for him," Tucker said.

"Ready? How?"

"Anybody tell you about Faye?"

Harvey nodded. "I heard it. He was a damn' fool for trying."

"His funeral's tomorrow?" Tucker asked.

Again Harvey nodded. "I sent word in to ask Corbett to fix it up."

Tucker reached in his vest pocket and brought out a buckskin bag which he tossed alongside Olmsted's leg. "There's two hundred dollars in eagles in there. One hundred of it is yours."

Harvey, watching him, rubbed his bald head to chase off a fly and then said, "For what?"

Tucker pondered the question. "Did anybody tell you that there was a torn cavalry neckerchief in Faye's hand when they found the body?"

"What does that mean?"

"The neckerchief belonged to Giff Ballew. A dozen people had seen him wearing it."

"You mean him and Faye fought and he gunned Faye?"

"That's the way it looks, and that's what Corbett thinks."

"Didn't know Faye knew Ballew," Harvey observed.

"That," Tucker said quietly, "is what the one hundred dollars is for. To improve your memory."

Harvey was watching carefully as Tucker went on. "Ballew rode out here to your place three days ago. He wanted you and Faye to throw in with him in a big raid on Circle W cattle. You told him you wanted nothing to do with it, that you were afraid of us. But Faye was still mad about getting caught skinning out one of our cows and losing his horse to Dad. Besides,

he was still mad about the hike to town. He agreed to
throw in with Ballew. They argued about the split and
finally Ballew agreed to the short end of it. He didn'
like it much but he agreed." Tucker paused. "All righ
so far?"

"Go on."

"That's the story you'll tell Corbett and that you'l
tell at the funeral and afterward at Carmody's Saloon
That's for the one hundred dollars."

Harvey hesitated. "You said two hundred is in th
poke."

"That's money you'll put up at Carmody's bar. It'
a reward for the capture of Giff Ballew, dead or alive
Remember that 'dead or alive' business."

Harvey said drily, "Corbett knows I ain't seen tha
much cash money in ten years."

"You've already sold three of Faye's horses to rais
the reward cash. You didn't need them and you wante
more than anything to nail down your brother's killer.'
He waited. "What about it?"

Harvey looked off at the horizon and was silent :
moment. Tucker wondered if he was considering forcin
Circle W to raise the ante, then surprisingly Harve
said, "Sure, sure."

Tucker stood up. "It beats rustling, doesn't it, Harv?'
Harvey nodded and looked gravely at Tucker. "Th
trouble is I've run out of brothers."

When Giff rounded the bend in the road to Harmony
that hid Dry Wells from sight, he pulled his horse of
the road and put him up the ridge. Reining in jus
below it, Giff climbed up the ridge, bellied down and
watched the stage station. *That was too close,* he
thought, and he felt a sudden gratitude to Hannah fo
her warning.

Now he saw Kelsey come out followed by Tucke
Weybright. After some conversation they both entere
the saloon door. Giff waited another two minutes ir
which he saw Kate Miles drive the buggy out from
under the cottonwoods and head up the Harmony

road, but there was no other activity. Apparently Tucker
had assumed that pursuit was useless.

He let Kate Miles pass below him, then mounted,
crossed over the ridge and put his bay in the direction
of Harmony. If Lynch Weybright had gone to Sheriff
Corbett with the yellow neckerchief, then it was only
wisdom to keep off the traveled roads. If Corbett believed
Lynch's story, and he had to, then Corbett would be
hunting him.

Who had put his neckerchief in Faye Olmsted's
hands? There was only one answer to that because only
Tucker Weybright and himself knew the location of
the neckerchief. It was a clever frame-up, Giff conceded
wryly. It would put not only Corbett and the law
against him, but when it became known it would put
the Breaks men against him too. It seemed to Giff then
that nothing worse could happen to him than had already happened, unless it was to walk into an ambush.

He wondered now if Kate Miles had really believed
he killed Faye Olmsted. He couldn't tell from her at-
titude there in the dining room if she thought him the
killer Weybright made out. Certainly his admission of
shooting a Circle W hand and his explanation of the
necessity for it hadn't impressed her. Perhaps he could
count one more person against him after this visit to
Dry Wells.

Now he put his attention to his next move. If he
could see Sheriff Corbett and explain the circumstances
under which he had lost the yellow neckerchief he
might be able to neutralize the sheriff. He doubted
this, since everyone from Kate Miles to Hannah Moore
conceded that Corbett was Weybright's man. Still the
evidence of the neckerchief was wholly circumstantial
and any sheriff, bought or not, should be reluctant to
go after a man on evidence that could have been so
easily framed.

Getting to see the sheriff was another thing. If he
rode into town he risked some Circle W rider or some
Breaks hothead shooting at him. Then a solution came
to him, and he wondered if he should take a chance.

He had done nothing but take chances so far and he was still alive, so he figured he might as well take this chance. When he pulled out of the Breaks onto grass lands in late afternoon, he stopped for an hour to let his horse graze its fill. The last few days had gaunted his bay and Giff had been unable to get grain for him.

Thus it was long after dark when Giff picked up the few lights of Harmony. As he rode into town he saw there were a few horses racked in front of Carmody's Saloon, but when he crossed Main Street it was almost deserted save the clutter of horses at the First Chance's tie-rail. Giff crossed the street and now realized he faced a dilemma. He couldn't put his horse up at the livery because it was just possible he would need him in a hurry. Nor could he tie him to one of the street racks where his brand might be recognized and the alarm given. He compromised this by turning into the first alley on his right where he tied his bay to the post of a store's loading platform.

Coming out of the alley, he achieved the plankwalk and turned down toward Main Street. When he came to the stairway that led up to Parry's office he turned to climb the stairs. In the darkness above he tried the door of Parry's waiting room and found it locked. Backing off, he raised a foot and kicked at the lock. The door burst open with a crash and he waited, listening to see if the noise attracted any attention from the street.

When he could hear nothing he closed the door behind him and moved across the room, memory telling him where the couch was placed. In a matter of seconds he was asleep on it.

It must have been because of the dark, windowless room that Giff slept so late. He came awake to hear a measured step on the stairway and now he came off the couch and moved over behind the door. When the door into Parry's office proper was open there would be light in this room, but now it was dim, with only a crack of daylight showing under the office door.

There was a noise of a key being inserted in the lock,

a mild cursing, and then the door swung open. A figure moved into the dark room and another key was inserted in the door leading into the office. As the door swung open the room flooded with light and the gray-haired lawyer was framed in the doorway. Now he turned back to see what had happened to the lock and saw Giff beside the door. Parry halted abruptly. "I broke in last night, Mr. Parry. I'll be glad to pay for having your lock fixed."

Parry was silent a moment. "But why break in at all?"

"I didn't reckon the hotel or the streets, the bars, or the livery stable were very healthy places for me to be seen."

"No," Parry agreed quietly. "I understand. Won't you come in?" He went into the office and Giff followed.

He was waved into the same chair he had sat in before, and he watched as Parry seated himself, tilted back in his chair and looked at him.

"What time is it, Mr. Parry?"

"Ten o'clock."

Giff smiled faintly and rubbed the bristles on his jaw. In the stillness it made a grating sound. Then Giff realized that to Parry he must seem a rough-looking customer.

"You must have wanted to see me badly. About what, I can't imagine," Parry offered.

"If you think a little, you will," Giff said slowly. "I'm in trouble, not only with Circle W but with the law."

Parry nodded. "If you're about to say what I think you are, I am unable, under the circumstances, to represent you."

"That's not what I was thinking. I wondered if you'd be fair enough to get Sheriff Corbett up here so I can talk with him?"

The lawyer frowned. "I imagine if you waited in the courthouse he'd come back to his office. I think he's at Faye Olmsted's funeral now."

"I'd like a witness to our conversation."

"But why me?"

"Because I think you're honest," Giff said quietly.

The older man smiled faintly. "That's strange, coming from you."

Giff said nothing, but let it rest at that. Parry turned, looked out the window for a moment and then nodded, rose and went over to the window beyond his desk and raised it. Leaning both hands on the window sill he scanned the street and presently called, "Oh, Sammie." He reached in his pocket for a coin, pitched it out the window and called, "Find Sheriff Corbett and bring him to my office, will you?"

The treble voice of a small boy answered, "Right away, Mr. Parry."

Parry turned away and sat down, and now he eyed Giff speculatively. "You seem to have got yourself into considerable confusion since I last saw you."

Giff nodded. "If that's the right word, I have."

"I'm sorry about that," Parry said, and Giff thought he meant it. "With other people and in a different part of the country, I think you might have had a chance."

"With different people," Giff underlined drily.

"I asume you don't want to talk until Corbett arrives. Is that right?" When Giff nodded, Parry said, "Then if you'll excuse me, I have some papers to attend to. Sit here if you wish, or maybe you'll find a more comfortable chair in the other room."

Giff rose and moved out into the reception room. If his plan was to work he would have had to move in to this room eventually anyway. Parry had provided the opportunity. There was always a chance that Parry had a gun hidden in his desk, but somehow Giff doubted this; also he doubted that Parry would use it if he did have one.

Giff prowled the room, studying titles of the law books, looking at the few pictures and the one framed map of San Dimas County. He was mentally tracing his route of the last few days on the map when he heard muffled footsteps on the stairway.

Now Giff moved over behind the door. Parry working at his desk, his back to the reception room, paid no attention. Whoever was climbing achieved the landing and Giff heard footsteps approaching.

Now the door opened and a man stepped through and began to swing the door shut. A look at his broad back told Giff he was a stocky man. Giff moved forward a step and swiftly lifted the man's gun from its holster. The man whirled as Giff took two steps backward. He did not raise the man's gun nor did he draw his own.

The first thing Giff remarked was the worn star on the vest of Sheriff Corbett. His was a swarthy face and his full lips seemed loose, his dark eyes pouched and sad with years of dissolute living. He didn't seem surprised or even particularly concerned as he half-turned to look at Parry who had come out of his chair and stood in the doorway.

"I never figured you for this, Parry. Him maybe, but not you." He trailed a plume of whiskey aroma as he moved forward.

"Rubbish!" Parry snorted. "Ballew wanted to talk with you in my presence. Removing your gun is only a sensible precaution. If he walked armed into your office you'd have removed his."

"In a hurry," Sheriff Corbett agreed. Even his voice seemed a little sad to Giff.

"Come into my office, won't you? Both of you."

Corbett preceded Giff and slacked into the chair that Giff had used, and Parry swung a straight-back chair from the opposite wall, gestured for Giff to sit down and then sat down himself.

Corbett said to Giff, "Lynch said not to bother to hunt you. You'd come to me. I didn't figure it would be here, though." He paused and sighed, "Go ahead."

"I understand Lynch also brought a yellow neckerchief in to you. It was found on the dead body of Faye Olmsted."

"By Will Overton. He's got no connection with Bib S or Circle W."

"You've identified it as mine?" Giff asked.

"It hasn't got your initials on it or anything like

that," the sheriff said, quiet derision in his voice. "Still, a half-dozen people have remembered that you wore one like it."

"It's mine, all right," Giff said.

Corbett looked at him sharply. "You admit it?"

"I admit it's my neckerchief. I don't admit quarreling with Faye Olmsted or shooting him."

"Then how did your neckerchief get in his hand?"

Giff leaned forward, elbows on knees, cradling the sheriff's gun in his hands. "The first day I got into town I went out to the Circle W. I was shown off the ranch by Tucker Weybright. We had a fight and Tucker tried to choke me by grabbing my neckerchief and twisting it. The neckerchief ripped in two. When I finished the fight it was on the ground underfoot. Since it was torn in two and useless, I walked away from it."

Parry had been watching Giff intently and now his glance shuttled to the sheriff.

Giff said, "Does that suggest anything to you, Sheriff?"

"What should it?"

"Only two people knew where that torn neckerchief was. I was one, Tucker Weybright was the other."

The sheriff pursed his full lips and looked at the ceiling. "I'll concede you had a fight, and I'll concede you lost your neckerchief, but the man you fought with was Faye Olmsted and it was over the division of the cattle you were rustling and would rustle."

Parry said quietly, "You must have a reason for saying that, Ed."

Speaking almost tonelessly, the sheriff, not looking at Giff, but at Parry, said, "Ballew rode out to the Olmsteds' place three days ago and wanted them to throw in with him rustling Circle W beef. Harvey thought the scheme was too dangerous. Faye was still riled up about getting caught rustling and having to deed over his horse to Lynch Weybright. Faye agreed to throw in with Ballew, but he wanted the big end of a seventy-thirty split. Ballew didn't like it, but he finally gave in. He and Faye were partners. The way I figure it, once they had the cattle started into the

Breaks they began rowing over the split." Now he looked at Giff. "You killed him. Isn't that so?"

"Where'd you get this information, Ed?" Parry asked.

"About the partnership? From Harv Olmsted. The rest speaks for itself, doesn't it?"

"Harv Olmsted is lying!" Giff said flatly. "I've never set eyes on the man. The only time I ever saw Faye Olmsted was in Carmody's Saloon!"

Now it was the sheriff's turn to lean forward. "Harv Olmsted is telling the truth," he said flatly. He paused. "He has deposited, at Carmody's Saloon, a hundred dollars in gold as a reward for your capture, dead or alive."

Parry said sharply, "When was this?"

"This morning. He'd sold three-four of Faye's horses to raise the money. Why would he offer a reward if he wasn't sure of the man who killed his brother?"

"Does your office hold with this reward idea, Ed?" Parry demanded. "It's plain head money. A man is putting up a hundred dollars to anyone who will kill another man for him."

"What's my office got to do with it?" Corbett countered. "I'm after Ballew on suspicion of murder. If he resists arrest, I'll shoot him."

"That's not the same thing," Parry said sharply. "You're an elected law officer. If you suspect Ballew of murder you have a right to capture him, question him, and if the evidence warrants, it's your duty to hold him without bail for trial. Anyone interferring with you is guilty of obstructing justice. If anyone shoots Ballew, he should be prosecuted."

"Why, I reckon he will be," Corbett said. "But that doesn't stop Harv Olmsted from paying a reward."

Giff interrupted drily. "You've got me dead already, and now you're discussing what to do with the man who shot me."

"I haven't got you dead," Corbett said. "It's Olmsted who's got you dead."

Giff smiled thinly, "Suppose I went over to Carmody's and posted a reward of a hundred dollars for anybody who would kill Harv Olmsted for me?"

"Harv isn't suspected of murder. You are," the sheriff said flatly.

Parry cut in sharply. "If you have any sense, Ed, you'll arrest Harv Olmsted. Ballew made a good point. Can anybody pay a hundred dollars to have another man killed?" Now Parry spoke with asperity. "It's perfectly proper to post a reward for the apprehension of a suspected criminal. *Apprehension,* I said. When it goes into this 'dead or alive' business, it's wrong and you know it. How can you give a man a fair trial when he's dead?"

"Look, the word's around." The sheriff shrugged his heavy shoulders. "Harv can deny he ever made the offer, but the offer's there."

Now Giff stood up. "See what I meant about a witness, Mr. Parry?" He looked at the sheriff, who was regarding him with sad and cynical eyes. "I asked Mr. Parry to bring you up here so I could point out to you where I left that neckerchief. I've found you've chosen to believe Olmsted's lies instead of the truth."

"If you told the truth, why don't you give yourself up, stand trial and prove the truth?"

Giff looked at Parry. "As a lawyer, would you advise that?"

Parry said drily, "Only for one reason. It would keep you from getting shot in the back before your trial."

"Do you think I'd get justice in a trial?"

The flush on Parry's face was plain as he said, "We like to think all men get justice in a court of law."

"Weybright's justice," Giff murmured. "With the evidence already carpentered for the frame. No thanks."

He turned and moved into the reception room, tossing the sheriff's gun on the couch as he passed it. He had his hand on the door handle when he heard Parry behind him. The lawyer came up to him and said quietly, "Just a minute, Ballew." He halted and said quietly, "You see what you're facing. Go home while you can."

"With a murder warrant out for me? You're talking to the wrong man, Mr. Parry. You may be concerned about me, but all you're doing is suggesting another way to get me off Weybright's back. I like it there."

He opened the door, still looking at Parry, and now as the door opened he saw a look of startled wonderment on Parry's face. Swiveling his head, Giff saw a tall man wearing a deputy's badge standing in the doorway, gun drawn, and scarcely four inches from his belly.

"Back up!" the man said curtly.

Giff took a step backward which brought him alongside Parry, on the lawyer's right, and the tall man took a step forward into the room.

Then he extended his left hand to lift Giff's gun from its holster. At that moment Parry slashed out at the tall man's gun arm, bringing both hands down on it, and at the same time he yelled, "Get out!" Giff's gun was already out of its holster when the tall man's gun went off. Giff felt something slam with a murderous force into his left thigh half-spinning him, and then he raised his gun and brought the barrel down across the tall man's temple. He fell slackly and Giff rushed through the door. His left leg almost gave under him, but he pushed away from the wall, wheeled into the stairwell and took two steps befor he saw the man on the steps below him silhouetted against the street. The man's gun was drawn, and now Giff, desperate, flattened himself against the wall as the man's gun went off.

Giff shot carefully then and watched as the man was slammed backward, lost his balance, fell and skidded down the few steps to the landing.

Now the pain came and Giff felt the wetness on his leg. Ignoring the throbbing ache, Giff took the steps two at a time, vaulted over the prone man, holstered his gun, and then in no particular haste, he turned out into the street and up toward the alley. Wrenching off his hat he held it in his left hand over his wound which he knew was bleeding and could be spotted by someone on the walk. Already a couple of men had halted in the middle of the street and were looking around uncertainly for the direction of the gun shots.

The plankwalk was crowded at this hour and now Giff, his jaws locked against the agony of his leg, moved upstreet. He was sure that no bone was broken since his left leg would hold its share of his weight, but he also knew that it would only be seconds before the hue and cry was on.

Before he reached the alley he came to the gray realization that even if he could make his horse and mount it he must give his leg attention or he would bleed to death.

A team pulling a spring wagon came out of the alley and turned upstreet into the morning traffic. The wagon's reach extended a couple of feet beyond the bed which was piled high with household goods and furniture. The driver, hunched over his reins, did not even look at Giff as he pulled out of the alley into the street.

With cool desperation Giff waited until the wagon passed him and then grasped the tail gate and sat down on the wagon's reach, feet trailing carelessly. He hoped that to the passing teams and passers-by he would appear to be a lazy adult hooking a children's ride on a passing wagon.

The piled goods hid him from the driver and now, as they pulled past the corner, Giff knew that this was only temporary respite. It was true that a wagon pulling in behind him hid him from the immediate view of the men who were bound to gather at Parry's stairwell, but the alert would be out in minutes.

Now he was passing the *San Dimas Times* and he had a desperate impulse to seek shelter there, but it was only an impulse; the *Times* would be the first place Corbett would look, since Sam had been friendly enough to accept his advertisement. Hiding there would only bring down Weybright's immediate suspicion and, upon discovery, his wrath on these two people who befriended him.

But he had to do something. His boot was filling with blood and now that they were getting out of the town's heaviest traffic he knew that he would become conspicuous perched on the wagon reach. The following wagon bed turned off into a side street. Each jolt of the wagon frame sent a new fire through his thigh and he knew with a gray certainty that he could not take this much longer.

Now the wagon was abreast the courthouse and, seeing it, a sudden and dangerous idea came to Giff. The sheriff's office was in the courthouse. The search for him would doubtless be directed from there. Why not hide in the least likely place, right under the noses of his hunters? He remembered the Land Office and old Rodney Allen. He also remembered the vault in Allen's office. Only Allen would have access to it.

Bracing himself now, Giff stepped off the wagon's reach and promptly sprawled on his face. Pulling himself upright, he looked about him to see if anyone had witnessed his fall. A pair of strolling women the wagon had just passed were so engrossed in their chatter that they did not even look at him. Then Giff measured the distance to the basement entrance of the register's office. He knew it would be the longest sixty yards he had ever walked and he would have to make the walk look natural and inconspicuous.

Still holding his hat against his leg, he started out, fighting his instinct to limp and ease his leg. The pain was fiery and constant and his progress painfully slow, but he managed to look like some aimless strolling stranger with no particular business on his mind. At the steps where no one could see him he skipped down the risers on his good leg, moved through the doorway and turned left into the open door of the Land Office. Old Rodney Allen looked up from his desk, smiled when he saw Giff, rose and came over to the counter.

Giff said quietly, but urgently, "Mr. Allen, I've got a fresh bullet hole in my leg. They're looking for me now or soon will be. Nobody has seen me come in here. Can I hide in your vault?"

It took only seconds for Allen to comprehend what Giff had asked. Giff wouldn't have blamed him for refusing help and he watched desperately as understanding came into the old man's face.

"Come through the gate," Allen said, moving toward it. Gratefully Giff limped through the gate and followed Allen into the dark vault. Allen pulled the door almost shut, then struck a match and lighted the lamp that sat on the square table. Then he toed a chair away from the table so that Giff could sit down.

The process of seating himself was exquisite agony and Giff broke out in a rush of drenching perspiration.

"Let's look at the leg," Allen said.

Giff lifted his hat from his thigh and now for the first time he looked at his wound. It was welling bright, crimson blood and Giff could feel it warm and puddling in his boot. The whole side of his trousers were dark with it where the street dust from his fall hadn't muddied it.

"Take off your belt, wrap it around your leg above the hole and I'll pull it tight," old Allen said swiftly.

Giff managed to get the belt off and Allen deftly wrapped it twice around his leg above the wound and cinched it securely. Afterward Allen straightened up and regarded Giff soberly.

"You're in trouble with that leg," he said. "We've got to stop the bleeding."

"Don't go for a doctor," Giff said. "They'll be watching him wherever he goes, and following him."

"Do they know you're hurt?"

"I think so."

The old man thought a moment. "I'm going to leave you," he said abruptly. "I'm going to lock you in here. I'll be back before you can breathe up all the air. Just rest a minute."

He went out and now Giff folded his arms on the table and cradled his head on them. The pain in his leg was constant but bearable, now that he was no longer walking or riding in a jolting wagon. But the pain was the least of his troubles, he knew. He couldn't stay here and he couldn't ask Allen to run the risk of helping him further.

Now, with bitter realization, he knew where he had made his mistake. He'd been warned indirectly by Corbett and he had been either too tired or too stupid to draw the logical conclusion from the sheriff's statement. Hadn't Corbett said, *"Lynch said not to bother to hunt you, you'd come to me?"* If the sheriff had acted on Lynch's advice, naturally he would never allow himself to be caught alone. Without suspecting what awaited him in Parry's office, he, nevertheless, had had the caution to post his men outside Parry's door and stairs in case Giff sought him out. Giff had got what he wanted from Corbett with Parry as a witness, but at what cost to himself.

Now he assessed his chances of escaping the town and he recognized, with a dismal certainty, that they were not good. As soon as his horse was discovered and as soon as Corbett could check on whether a horse had been stolen, the sheriff would be fairly certain that Giff was hiding out somewhere in Harmony. Inevitably, perhaps at the very end of their search, they would want to look in the vault of the Land Office. But even if he left here, and he must, where could he go?

The next thing he knew his shoulder was being shaken and he roused from a sleep of exhaustion to see old Allen and Sam Furman standing beside him. He straightened up. Sam said softly, "You damn' fool! Don't you know the sheriff's office is at the other end of the basement?"

Giff nodded wearily. "That's why I came here."

"That's why I took him in, too," Allen said. "Anybody smart enough to hide under their noses deserves some help." He nodded to Sam. "I knew Sam liked you, so I brought him."

He lifted a pint bottle of whiskey from his coat pocket, pulled out the cork and said, "Get some of that down."

Giff obeyed and felt the fiery jolt of the whiskey put a new, if temporary, energy into his weary body. His leg was dangerously numb and he knew that he would have to uncinch the tourniquet. He glanced up at Sam and said, "You shouldn't be here, Sam."

Sam's lean face was both troubled and scared, but when Giff finished he only shook his head. "I'm in Rodney's office three or four times a week after legal descriptions. If we're seen together they'll think it's business."

Now the old man came around the table and put a paper sack on it. "Now let's get at that leg."

He loosened the belt and gently slipped Giff's trousers down below the wound which began to bleed afresh through the bruised puncture. Allen took the sack and poured its contents liberally on the bleeding wound.

"What is it?" Giff asked.

"Plain flour," Allen said. "With any luck it'll cake and stop the bleeding." He then took a new store-bought bandanna, poured flour into it and pressed it against the torn flesh where the bullet had come out. Now he took another new handkerchief from his pocket and, while he held the crude poltice in place, Sam bound the wound with the clean cloth.

Finished, with Giff's trousers belted back around him, old Allen tilted his head toward the whiskey bottle and said, "Take another drink. Come to think of it, I'll help you."

Giff took another drink and passed the bottle to the old man who helped himself to a long pull, then passed it to Sam who only shook his head in refusal.

Now the two men, both with troubled expressions on their faces, regarded him.

"What's Corbett doing, Sam?" Giff asked.

"What do you think?" Sam said bitterly. "They found your horse, but they figure you might have taken a closer one. Corbett's sent word out to the Circle W. He's going to deputize Stoughton's crew and Weybright's."

"Do they think I'm still in town?"

"They can't find anybody who saw you ride out. They don't know, but they think you're hurt."

"What's going to happen, Sam?" Giff asked wearily.

"If Corbett can't find anybody who saw you ride out he says he'll search house to house." Sam grimaced. "I think that's why he's deputizing the two crews. If anybody objects to a house-to-house search they'll be arguing with a couple of dozen men."

"Can you get me a horse, Sam?"

"Don't be a fool!" Sam said angrily. "Sure, I can get you a horse, but can you get on it and where are you going? There's a storm making up that looks like a good one. How will you eat? What happens if fever comes?"

Giff had no answer to these questions and he was silent.

Then Sam said, "I've got it figured out, Ballew. Stay here and sleep till dark, then I'll take you to my place."

Giff shook his head. "This is no trouble of yours. Besides, if I'm caught in your place you'll have Weybright and the law on you. They'd be rough."

"That's my risk," Sam said curtly. "Think you can make it a couple of blocks tonight?"

Giff hated the dilemma before him. To stay here, even if he could secretly be fed by Allen, would be to put the old man's safety in jeopardy. To go to Sam Furman's, where at least he could lie down and feed himself, would be to risk Sam's safety. *I could give myself up,* he thought in quiet despair, and then a new thought occurred to him.

"Did I kill the man on the stairs?"

"You smashed his arm. His fall backward knocked him out, that's all."

Then he had only one murder charge to face and that was a false one. He knew that Parry knew this too. If he could get past these next few days, he would be able to fight again. But right now he was too tired to think or reason. He looked up at Sam. "Suppose I make it to your place? Where do we go from there?"

"One thing at a time," Sam said drily.

Sam left then, and when he was gone old Allen said, "You sleep. I'll blow out the light and leave the door open a ways. Don't worry because nobody comes in here but me."

All Giff could say through the weariness that engulfed him was, "Thanks, old-timer."

He slept through the day and old Allen, when he closed up for the day, did not bother to wake him, knowing that Giff would need all his remaining strength for the journey to Furman's.

Giff was still sleeping in the dark vault, head cradled on his arms, when Sam roused him in the darkness.

"No lights," Sam said in greeting. "Can you stand up?"

Giff sat motionless a moment in the stillness and

presently said, "Give me your arm." When he groped for Sam's arm and found it, he felt a wetness on Sam's coat. He realized then it was a slicker beneath his hand and he asked, "It's raining?"

"Like the devil," Sam said, satisfaction in his voice. "I've got a slicker for you and a cane. Now hoist yourself up, son."

Giff came to his feet with an effort and shrugged into the slicker Sam had brought. The cane, when he tested it, was a real help in taking the weight off his throbbing leg. Now he felt Sam grope for his hand and a bottle was placed in it. "Drink it all. This is medicine."

It was the remainder of Allen's whiskey and Giff gagged it down.

"Put an arm around me," Sam said. "If we meet anybody, give me the cane and pretend you're drunk." Sam chuckled softly, "You just might be, at that. Now let's go."

They went through the dark office and up the stairs and Giff felt a lightheadedness that he knew came from the whiskey. Outside it was raining steadily and Sam steered him across the courthouse yard and across the muddy road. There was scarcely a lamp lighted and Giff guessed that this was an early morning hour Sam had chosen for the journey so that the town would be asleep.

With frequent rests to ease his throbbing leg, they slowly made their way to the edge of town, meeting nobody, and turned down a dark alley that ran alongside a frame house. Attached to it and at its rear was a lean-to of logs, and Sam steered Giff through the door that opened onto the alley. Once inside, Sam propped Giff against the wall while he lighted the lamp. Giff noted with utter indifference that this room was a kitchen-living room.

Now Sam, carrying a lamp, led him through into the bedroom where he peeled off Giff's coat before he steered him to the bed in the corner of the small room. The exhaustion of his journey and a rising fever made Giff totally indifferent to his surroundings. He let Sam pull off his boots and gently push him down. He felt the blanket being thrown over him and heard Sam say, "I was going to feed you, but you're too tired to hold a fork. Go to sleep, old son."

It was a command Giff could not have disobeyed if he wanted to.

Sam, standing over him, watched and listened to his quick and ominous breathing. Then Sam said softly, "You poor, miserable, magnificent, indestructible bastard."

Chapter Six

IT WAS raining steadily and hard when Kate drove her buggy into the livery runway. From her lap she lifted the rain apron that Prudencio had fastened to the splashboard this morning, tilted the pooled water from it and then removed the lap robe from around her legs. The hostler lifted her down and handed her the umbrella from the seat, saying, "Don't worry, Mrs. Miles, I'll wipe the little mare down good."

"This rain should bring a foot of grass, so we can't complain, Bert," Kate said pleasantly.

"No ma'm, but you'd better stick to the planks crossing the street or we're apt to lose you."

Kate turned away and then halted, turned back and asked the hostler, "Is there any news about this Ballew fellow?"

"Nothing new," Bert said. "They reckon he's hiding in town though."

"If he isn't, they'll have a fine time tracking him

in this, won't they?" Kate said, just for something to say.

Bert chuckled. "That bunch will do all their tracking in a saloon, you can bet that."

Kate turned away, put up her umbrella and stepped out onto the rainy plankwalk. She hoped the relief at hearing that Ballew was still free didn't show in her face. *Lord knows, it's haggard enough,* she thought. She had slept little last night, haunted by the possibility that Sam had been unsuccessful in getting Giff to his house. The fact that Giff's wound had received no attention troubled her too. Perhaps she could go over this morning with medicines and bandage it properly.

She turned at the corner and, in passing the steps to Parry's office, she looked inside. The brown stain of dried blood from the man Giff had wounded was still there, and she wondered again by what miracle Giff had managed to escape this ambush. He'd been a fool to come to town, but, according to Sam who had got it from Parry, Giff had wanted to put Parry and Corbett right about his neckerchief that was found in Olmsted's hand. If he had an alibi it was strange he hadn't told her when she mentioned the neckerchief at the Dry Wells stage station. There really wasn't much friendliness in the man, she thought, but he had a kind of reckless daring that at times was appalling. His visit to Circle W had been foolhardy, but his selection of a place to hide after he was shot bordered on insanity, she thought, and thinking it she couldn't help but admire his courage. Nor could she help but compare him with Dan Miles, that weak and cowardly man who had once been her husband.

The streets were a mire and already the planks that had been laid from corner to corner were either floating in puddles or had been mashed into the mud by wagon traffic. Only people with the most urgent errands were on the streets today, she noticed. When she reached the corner above the *Times* office it was surprising, therefore, to see two riders in slickers idling on the plankwalk in front of the *Times*. She moved on up to them and recognized one of them, Con Hart, a Circle W rider. She nodded to him and he touched his hat. She twisted the knob of the office door. It turned, but the door did not give; it was locked.

Something's happened, she thought in swift panic. In all the time she had worked for Sam Furman he had always been at work before she arrived. Holding her umbrella handle under one arm, she rummaged in her purse for the shop key and unlocked the door. Then she closed her umbrella and stepped inside and began to shut the door behind her. It did not close and she looked around. Con Hart was standing in the doorway, holding it open, and now he stepped in, followed by his companion.

Kate put her umbrella in the corner and said, "Anything I can do for you, Con?"

"We want to look through your place."

Kate frowned, "What for?"

"We're searching the whole town for Ballew. He's hid here somewhere."

A sudden anger came to Kate. "You'll do no searching here without Sam Furman's permission! And he's not here yet."

Patiently Hart, who was a tall, mournful-looking man, unbuttoned his slicker, reached in his vest pocket and took out a folded piece of paper. With his other hand he dug into his trousers pocket and pulled out a badge which he showed in his palm.

"This is a search warrant, Mrs. Miles, and this here is my deputy's badge."

Kate looked at neither the badge nor the warrant. She was sure that Corbett would have made this legal.

"How long have you been a deputy, Con?" Kate asked slowly.

"Since this morning." Con's look was faintly sheepish.

"Along with how many others?"

"Around twenty, I reckon."

Kate lifted her shoulders in a shrug. "Go ahead and search."

Con moved past her, heading for the shop; then he spied the big wardrobe in the corner. Lifting his gun from its holster he moved over to the wardrobe and pulled the door open. The door, as was its nature, came off its hinges and rapped Con smartly across the head before it fell to the floor.

Suppressing a wicked satisfaction, Kate said, "Does your search warrant include wrecking the place?"

Swearing softly, Hart put the door back in place, then he and his companion moved back into the shop. This, Kate knew, was a grimly serious business. If these twenty men Hart had mentioned were going through the town searching every building, then Giff Ballew was certain to be caught. Surely they would not exclude Sam's place in their search. She knew that she must get word to him immediately.

Moving over to the door she watched the two men prowling the dark shop, looking into cupboards, under work tables and even peering into the presses. When they reached the rear wall they turned and came back.

Kate stepped out of the doorway and Con Hart, not looking at her, said, "Thanks, Mrs. Miles."

Kate allowed two minutes for them to be on their business elsewhere, then picked up her umbrella, opened the door and peered out into the street. They had vanished. Now she pulled the door closed behind her, opened her umbrella and retraced her steps to the livery. She made herself hold to an unhurried pace, not wanting to arouse suspicion.

At the livery Bert was lounging in the doorway. When she stepped inside, Bert looked at her in puzzlement.

"I've got the day off, Bert. I don't know why Sam made me drive all the way to town in this weather to tell me."

"Want me to hook up?"

"Since a woman can't spend her off day in a saloon I think you'd better."

Bert laughed and turned back into the stable.

Kate wished the sick feeling of apprehension inside her would go. What was Sam going to do with Ballew? Even if he could move, where would he move to? Her attention was directed at the hotel veranda across the street. Tucker Weybright, with two men trailing him, stepped off the veranda into the rain, turned right and entered Cunningham's Hardware Store. They were part of the search party, Kate supposed, and she thought of Tucker Weybright with a bitter hatred. If it hadn't been for him and his father neither Giff, Sam, Hannah, or herself would be in the positions they were in. The Weybrights were a blight on the country, she thought.

She heard the buggy approach and Bert dropped down from the buggy step and handed her up, afterward giving her the reins. She pulled the ample rain apron over her lap and around her legs to protect her against the driving rain.

Bert said, "See you tomorrow, Mrs. Miles," and whacked Kate's mare affectionately across the rump. Kate drove out into the rain, turned right and then right again at the corner. There was no reason to hide her visit to Sam, she thought. It would be natural enough for Con Hart, even if he saw her, to assume she was hunting up Sam to tell him of the unwarranted search.

The streets were almost empty and the steady rain was dimpling every pool. Passing the courthouse she turned right, drove two blocks, past small frame houses and log cabins, pulled into the alley and drew up at Sam's door.

Lifting the rain apron from her lap, a sudden thought came to her and she felt her heart pounding in wild excitement.

Why not? she thought. She moved the rain apron off her lap, stepped down into the rain and knocked on Sam's door. There was no answer and she tried the knob. The door was locked, but she had an intuitive feeling that Sam was inside. She called softly, "It's me, Sam, Kate. Open up!"

Immediately she heard the lock turn and Sam swung the door open just wide enough for her to slip through. He closed the door behind him and she saw the gun in his hand.

"How is he?" Kate asked.

"Fever," Sam said grimly.

"Do you know they're searching the town for him,

Sam? They've already been to the shop and they'll come here. Twenty of them are deputized and they have search warrants."

"I know," Sam said. "They were here earlier and beat on the door. I guess they figured I was at the shop, but they'll be back."

Kate said, matter-of-fact, "We've got to move him, Sam."

"Move him?" Sam's voice was bitter. "How can we move him in daylight? Where do we move him to?"

"We move him to my place."

Sam only stared at her for a moment, then he said sourly, "Sure, sure. How do we move him?"

"In my buggy."

"You think they won't spot him sitting there beside you?"

"Sam, I've got the rain apron on. We can put him on the floor. When I cover him with my blanket and pull the rain apron over my lap nobody can see him."

Sam frowned. "He's too big for that space."

"I don't think so, Sam. There's an open space between the seat and the floor of the bed. We can run his legs under the seat into the box and cover them."

Sam nodded. "I'll go with you."

"That's no good," Kate said. "If they see us together driving out of town, they'll wonder why you're not at work. They're used to seeing me alone."

"You're right," Sam said, and then he reached out and took Kate's hand. "Katie, you're a wonder. You know what you're getting into if you're discovered."

"They don't shoot women," Kate said tartly. "Not even the Weybrights. Now let me see him."

Sam moved ahead of her into the bedroom. Giff lay under the blanket still in his clothes, his eyes bright with fever. When he saw Kate, he smiled and his teeth were a startling white against the dark beard stubble of his cheeks. His gun lay on the blanket. At sight of him, Kate's heart seemed to melt inside her. This big man, strong enough to defy two dozen men, was now as helpless as a child.

"Excuse me for not getting up," Giff said weakly.

Sam said from beside Kate, "They're turning over the town, Giff. They'll be back here sure as you're born when they discover I'm not at work. We're moving you."

"To where?" Giff asked.

"Keefer's."

Giff's feverish glance shuttled to Kate. "You're the one who didn't want any part of this, Mrs. Miles," he said.

"I changed my mind," Kate said. "Besides Dad would never forgive me if I didn't help you."

"Do you know what it means if I'm found at your place?"

"Better than you do," Kate said. "It doesn't matter."

"How do I get out there?"

Sam explained to Giff about Kate's buggy with its rain apron that would hide him on the floor. Giff listened and, at the end, nodded. He seemed strangely meek, Kate thought, and then she realized that he had no other choice but to accept. He was not only at the mercy of his enemies, but also was at the mercy of his friends.

Now Sam rolled back the blanket and he and Kate pulled Giff to his feet. While he put his weight on Kate, Sam guided one arm and then the other into a heavy overcoat whose sleeves caught Giff's arms far above the wrists.

Supported by the two of them and the cane, Giff hobbled to the doorway and leaned against the wall by it. Now Sam stepped out into the rain and backed the buggy against the doorway. Then, looking up and down the alley and seeing no one, Sam called softly, "Come ahead."

Giff moved past the threshold, leaned all his weight on the cane and put his good leg on the buggy step. It had to be guided by Kate, then Sam seized the shoulders of Giff's coat and hauled and guided him until he was on his knees on the buggy floor. Then Sam turned him on his side and began to gently work his legs under the seat. Sam knew he was hurting him and he saw great beads of perspiration on Giff's face, but there was no way to do it without hurting him. Finally Giff lay jackknifed on the buggy floor, his back against the splashboard, his legs under the seat and his feet lying flat in the box.

Now Sam gave Kate a hand up and then said, "Wait a minute, Katie."

He went back into the house and returned with a piece of tarp and with this he covered Giff's legs and boots. By the time he was finished Kate covered Giff with the blanket and then pulled the rain apron over Giff and onto her lap.

Sam, water streaming from his hair, circled the buggy, saw that Giff was not visible from either side and then returned to Kate and said quietly, "Don't stop for anybody."

Kate nodded and put her mare into motion down the alley, circling the two blocks she came back past the courthouse, the *Times* office, and crossed Main Street heading south out of town. When she had passed the last house she lifted the rain apron and called, "Are you all right?"

There was no answer and now Kate felt a moment of panic. Was he in delirium or had he fainted? She knew then that she could not haul him to a sitting position in the buggy. The thing to do was get him home and get there fast.

The search for Giff took two days. The second day of search was ordered by Tucker Weybright because Ballew had not been turned up the first day. It did not endear him to the citizens of Harmony. Indeed, a Circle W hand had been shot at with a Civil War musket by an irascible old-timer who resented having his cabin searched two days in a row.

On the second day of the search the rain fell even harder than the previous day. The roofs of two or three adobes at the outskirt of town had caved in and Sheriff Corbett, always a politician, had asked for and got money from the Weybrights to buy shelter and food for the two luckless families.

The sheriff's office was headquarters for the search group. Its stone floor was covered with a half-inch blanket of mud trailed in by the Weybright and Stoughton crews.

It was a little after the noon hour and Tucker Weybright, his slicker still dripping, was enjoying an after-dinner cigar. He was seated in the only comfortable chair in the office, a swivel chair at Corbett's desk. Corbett himself was unsteadily pacing the dirty floor. He had drunk his dinner in preparation for a new tongue-lashing from Tucker.

"How about attics?" Tucker demanded. "Every one of these frame houses has got an attic. Maybe there's a trap door in a closet or something, but there's always a trap door."

"I know," Corbett said. "I told them all to be sure and check on attics."

"Check, hell." Tucker's dark face was angry and scornful. "Did you *see* them do it?"

The sheriff stopped. "I can't be everywhere all the time, Tuck."

"He's here, I tell you!" Tucker said. He took the cigar from his mouth and leaned forward, his mouth open to speak. Then he heard footsteps coming down the basement stairs and swiftly approaching the sheriff's office.

Tucker looked up expectantly, hoping these men—for there was more than one—would bring him the news he was waiting for.

Then Todd Stoughton stepped into the room, followed by Lee Weybright. They both wore slickers and Todd Stoughton's pale eyes were dancing with anger.

"Tuck, I want my crew back."

"They're busy being deputy sheriffs," Tucker said drily. "What's the matter?"

"While you had both our crews beating up the town a bunch of those Breaks riffraff moved in on our beef."

Tucker slowly came out of his chair. "Any of ours?"

"I reckon," Stoughton said angrily. "Your stuff was with ours."

"When did this happen?"

"Sometime during the rain after you called our crews into town."

"Who's been at Carmody's?"

Lee spoke up then, "None of the Breaks bunch. I figured they were making themselves scarce so they wouldn't meet our crews."

"How do you know this?" Tucker demanded.

"Overton came around yesterday," Stoughton said. "He's been saving a couple of grassy canyons for late spring grazing. With this rain he figured he didn't need to save it any longer and when he pushed his stuff into it he found ours had drifted in. Maybe a hundred head. He had his men push them out of the canyon and head them west."

"Well?"

"I rode over this morning. Overton pushed them west all right, but somebody had kept on pushing them into the Breaks."

"Not Overton?"

"Not likely," Stoughton said curtly.

"And then what?" Tucker demanded.

"I followed the tracks into the Breaks, but the bunch was split up and the rain did the rest."

Tucker glared at him. "You can't hide a hundred head of cattle in that country."

"With two days and a night of this rain they could be on the other side of the San Dimas and wouldn't have left a track!" Stoughton said sharply. "I want my crew back."

"Take them," Tucker said angrily. "They haven't done me any good."

Stoughton turned to Sheriff Corbett. "Send them home when then show up, Sheriff," and he turned and tramped out.

"If we're being stolen blind, I'd better get back, Tuck," Lee said.

Tucker suddenly flung the remains of his cigar in the corner with a savage gesture. "No, Lee. They won't be trying it again. You come with me."

"Where?"

"Dry Wells. If Kelsey hasn't got a lead on who pulled this, I'll cut his other arm off."

Sheriff Corbett asked, "What about Ballew?"

"Dad can run the hunt from the hotel. Tell him where I've gone. Come on, Lee."

They tramped in the rain to the livery stable, picked up their mounts, then set out for Dry Wells. It was a miserable ride, cold and wet, and Tucker could not even keep a cigar going. Lee, Tucker noticed, looked silent and worried. Finally Tucker said brusquely, "What's eating you?"

Lee glanced at him through the streaming rain. "You really believe Ballew's in town?"

"How could he get out?"

"Then why didn't we find him?" Lee demanded.

"We will."

Lee watched him closely. "Then what happens, Tuck?"

"Why, he won't let himself be taken alive. You saw that when he broke out of Parry's office. Somebody will get him. There's that hundred dollars, you know."

"I know," Lee said softly, his voice empty of any feeling.

It was after dark when they picked up the lights of Dry Wells and both Lee and Tucker rode past the saloon where a lamp was lighted and headed for the corral. The stage horses were huddled out of the rain under an open-face shed and the Circle W horses joined them.

Now Lee and Tucker slogged through the mud toward the saloon. Tucker noticed that there was a light in Hannah's house, and he was remembering her defiance of him after he had almost run into Ballew. They rounded the corner of the building and Tucker stepped first through the door. Kelsey was seated on a high stool behind the rough bar, playing solitaire with a deck of worn cards. Because of his handless arm, he was shuffling the deck by endlessly cutting and he was so absorbed with this that Tucker and Lee were inside the room before Kelsey was aware of their presence.

"You really picked a night to ride, boys," he said, and slid off the stool. "Whiskey for you?"

Tucker nodded and came over to the bar, opening his dripping slicker. Lee moved down to the store end of the room, poked about, found some jerky and came back to the bar, chewing on a chunk of it.

By that time Tucker had had three fast drinks, and now he put both elbows on the mahogany and regarded Kelsey. "I want to know everything you know, Kelsey, about that raid on our beef."

"Everything I know is nothing," Kelsey said flatly.

Tucker smiled crookedly and his eyes held open disdain. "Nobody was in here today? Nobody talked?" He paused. "If they didn't talk, how did you know our beef had been driven off?"

"I didn't until you just now told me," Kelsey said. He frowned. "That explains something then."

Tucker waited.

"I've had maybe four customers today," Kelsey said. "All of them women for groceries. Yours is the first drink of whiskey I've sold today."

"They keeping away from you?" Tucker asked.

"Today, yes. Yesterday, no. Harv Olmsted was in to get liquored up and talk."

"What did he say?"

"That the reward money had come from you."

Lee swiftly looked up at Tucker with utter surprise in his young face. "Did it?"

Tucker nodded idly. "It had to come from somewhere. Harv didn't have it. Why not from us?" Tucker looked unflinchingly at Lee, and Lee's glance fell away.

"What difference does it make just as long as it gets us, Ballew?" Tucker asked irritably.

Then Hannah's voice came from the dining-room door and it was cold and accusing, "It makes plenty of difference."

Tucker lifted and turned his head to regard the girl, then he pushed away from the bar and slowly walked up to the dining-room doorway. "Go get us some grub," he said curtly. Without speaking Hannah turned, paused at the table to turn up the wick on the lamp and then went into the kitchen.

Tucker put the point of his shoulder against the kitchen doorframe and asked, "What difference?"

Hannah turned slowly. "You've done a lot of dirty things since I've known you, Tucker, but you've never paid to have a man bushwhacked."

Tucker frowned and he was honestly puzzled. "What's dirty about giving a man reward money to post for another man who's trying to ruin me and my family?"

"Why didn't you post it yourself?"

"It wasn't my brother Ballew killed."

"Nobody believes Ballew killed Faye," Hannah said hotly. "You see, none of it's worth it, Tucker. You don't understand these people." She went over to the stove and stirred up the coals, then put a skillet on the stove top.

Tucker was watching her in puzzlement. "Do I need to understand them?" he asked then, contempt in his voice.

Hannah turned and said slowly, "I think you do. Olmsted's reward offer didn't fool anybody. Nobody in this country has got money like that, least of all the Olmsteds. There is no cash money in this country. People trade for what they want for something they don't need as badly. Nobody would pay Harv Olmsted a hundred dollars for three horses. They'd trade but not pay money. Everybody knows you gave him the money."

"What if they do?"

"I don't know how Faye was killed or who killed him. He was probably rustling, but you'll get nobody here to believe it was Ballew."

"Why not? Harv's story to the sheriff was likely."

"It's what you would think was likely," Hannah said scornfully. "Ballew has been in this country twice. He didn't know it, but he was watched every minute. He never visited the Olmsteds. He never saw Harv. If you think you can buy his death for a hundred dollars from anyone around here, you're wrong."

"We'll see," Tucker said drily.

How Hannah threw in the floured steaks and poked them around with a fork. Her face, Tucker saw, held a strange and deep anger. Now he moved over and leaned against the counter where he could watch her. "Go on," he prodded.

Hannah looked up and gave him a level glance. "You poor fool. Ballew is fighting you and so are they! He can do things they can't! He's done them! They're fo him! You haven't fooled anybody by blaming Faye's death on him. They know better!"

Tucker shrugged. "You can't blame me for trying."

"But I do!" Hannah said bitterly. "We're through, Tucker! If you ever come in my house, and that means tonight, I'll shoot you. Tomorrow I'm leaving."

"For where?" There was a jeer in Tucker's voice.

"I heard Kelsey tell you there were only four women in here today. One of them was my married sister. She's the one who told me what these people thought of you and what you were trying to do to Ballew. I'm moving in with her."

Tucker straightened up. "Well, that'll save me some money."

"We won't need you, your daughter and me."

Tucker started to turn away, then halted and looked at Hannah. "You like this Ballew?"

"I like what he's doing to you Weybrights!" Hannah said, and there was almost a feral smile on her face. "I like what he'll keep on doing, too."

A sudden alertness came to Tucker's face, "You like him well enough to hide him?"

"Go look," Hannah snapped. "Take a last look at your daughter while you're there."

Now Lee stepped through the doorway and nodded at Hannah, who ignored him. Tucker, however, was standing motionless, regarding the back door. Hannah would hide him, Tucker knew. What if Ballew had got out of town someway? What would be so strange about him heading for Dry Wells, where, according to Hannah, the people around here liked him? Hannah could feed him and hide him. Was her invitation to him to look just a brassy dare?

Feeling foolish and angry at himself for feeling so, he moved toward the back door. He just would look.

When he had gone out Hannah busied herself preparing the meal, and Lee, his face troubled and almost shy, watched her. Presently he asked, "What's so wrong about the reward?"

Hannah stopped her work and half-turned. "I've got eleven dollars cash saved up. Do you think I should go in and leave it with Kelsey to be claimed by anyone who would kill you?"

"I've killed no kin of yours."

"Faye Olmsted was a cousin to me, a long way off, but still a cousin. It's much more likely you killed Faye than Ballew did, so what's wrong with my putting up that head money for you?"

When Lee did not answer, Hannah turned back to her work, and Lee, frowning, watched her. She was, he knew, from one of the families in the Breaks that had been fought off Circle W range. He had always been told that these were his enemies and that they must be kept down, but in a way she was right. If Harv Olmsted could post a reward for Ballew, she could post one for him, Lee. Still, there was evidence of a sort against Ballew and there was no evidence against him.

He shook his head in puzzlement. There was a line of reasoning here he couldn't follow. Hadn't he overheard Hannah Moore say that Ballew had been followed the two times he'd come into the Breaks and that he'd never met with Harv Olmsted?

Memory of that made him ask, "You don't think Harv Olmsted was telling the truth when he said Faye and Ballew were in partnership?"

"I think he said it for money," Hannah said drily. "He was in here and drunk yesterday. He was spending money he's never had before."

"Where'd he get it?"

"Anything I say would be a guess," Hannah said tonelessly.

"All right, guess."

Hannah looked directly at him. "I think you Weybrights gave it to him for that cock-and-bull story about Ballew that he carried to the sheriff." She picked up the plates. "Now, please step out of the way."

Lee stepped aside and Hannah went into the dining room. As she turned into the kitchen Tucker stepped through the door and shook the rain off his hat. He said nothing and Hannah said nothing, as he peeled out of his slicker, moved into the dining room and sat down opposite Lee.

Tucker hoped that the foolishness he felt did not show in his face. Hannah's clean rooms were empty save for the crib next to her bed where Lilly lay sleeping. He had been too suspicious and had made a fool of himself.

The brothers ate in silence. Hannah came in later with coffee and dried apple pie which she put before them. Afterward they heard her blow out the kitchen lamp and heard the door close.

When they were finished eating, Kelsey came in with a couple of blankets which he put on the bench beside Lee. "Reckon your blanket roll is soaked. You can bunk down here if you like."

Tucker said stonily, "Bring a pair for me." He saw Kelsey's eyes widen in surprise, and angrily Tucker stared him down.

It was the evening of the day after Kate had brought him to Keefer's that Giff's fever broke and he came awake and aware. Patiently he regarded the room. The lamp turned low on the bedside table, the two chairs, the rain-lashed windows and the clean, whitewashed adobe walls were strange to him.

He did not immediately know where he was, but as he pieced fever-weary memory together, he remembered Kate Miles and Sam Furman helping him out of the bed in Sam's cabin. There had been an urgency to move him. But where? He'd been standing on his feet between when memory ended.

Now he heard the door open softly and turned his head. The bulky body of Mike Keefer stood in the doorway. Keefer smiled, stepped back, called, "Kate, he's awake," and then came back into the room, walking up to the bed.

"So I'm at your place," Giff said. His voice was frail and quavering and he cleared his throat to give it some sort of timbre. "How'd I get here?"

"On the floor of Kate's buggy," Keefer said. He explained how Kate calmly hid him under the rain apron and drove out of town past the searchers. As he was finishing, Kate come into the room carrying a tray.

When she saw him she smiled. She put the tray on the table, and as she regarded him, some of the concern washed out of her eyes.

"See if you can haul yourself up so I can put this tray on your lap."

Giff put his arms under him and gently eased himself back against the headboard of the bed. He felt a bulky bandage around his leg in which, surprisingly, there was only a suggestion of pain. At the same time he was working himself into a sitting position he realized that he was ravishingly, overwhelmingly hungry.

Kate put the tray before him and said, "Talk later. Now, go ahead and eat."

There was a thick beef soup and freshly made bread on the tray, and Giff ate with a fierce gusto. He had eaten three bowls of the soup before he put down his spoon and accepted the cigar Keefer offered him.

"How long have I been here?" was Giff's first question.

"Since yesterday morning," Keefer said. "Do I need to add, you're welcome?" He fired up a cigar himself and pulled a chair over for Kate. She, however, sank down on the foot of the bed.

"If you're going to thank me for nursing you, don't. Dad managed to sit on you and pour water down your throat while I went to work."

Keefer said, "We were afraid they'd miss her."

Giff looked at Kate and smiled faintly. "I take it they haven't found Ballew yet."

Kate shook her head and smiled back. "They made a second house-to-house search today before it was called off. Both crews had to get back because their cattle were being driven off." She added, laughing, "Advertising in the *Times* always brings results, you see."

"What about Tucker?"

"When last seen he was foaming."

"Did they bother Sam?"

"They wanted to know where he'd been. He told them he'd been to the Land Office and old Mr. Allen covered for him."

Giff felt a vast relief at this news. Apparently his

escape had jeopardized nobody, except that it was jeopardizing Keefer and Kate right now. However, the chances of his being discovered here were remote, he thought. Once it was assumed he got away without leaving any kind of trail to follow it would be impossible to know where to look for him.

Now Kate stood up and said, "Dad, I think we should let him sleep now."

The warm food, and the absence of delirium had combined to make Giff so drowsy that he could barely keep his eyes open. Willingly he snuffed out his cigar and slid down under the covers as Keefer left the room. Kate turned the lamp low and said good night, but Giff was too drowsy to answer.

He slept deeply for a few hours and then came awake for no reason at all. He soon found that sleep would not return and he lay there staring at the ceiling, his thoughts reviewing what had happened. Thanks to the risks and kindness of four people—no five, for it was Parry who had made his escape possible—he was alive and mending. Still he was no nearer the goal he had set himself than the day he came. A little nearer perhaps, for Circle W was loosing cattle, but they would learn ways to control that and they still sat on land that was his.

He knew then that he would have to get moving and soon. He could not lie here and let events work themselves out. Curiosity came to him then and he wondered how close he was to being well.

Rising on an elbow, he turned up the lamp a bit and then threw back the covers. He was stripped to the waist and he saw that Keefer had provided him with a pair of his own underwear pants that hit Giff just below the knees. The bandage on his left thigh bulged under the cloth.

Swinging both feet to the floor, he gathered his strength and slowly pushed himself to his feet, holding onto the table beside the bed. Once erect, he distributed his weight evenly on both feet and found that he had no pain in his wound. Slowly then he took the first steps and now with movement he became aware of the wound. But still the leg held his weight momentarily and he set himself this midnight chore of circling the bed. It was slow work and sometimes painful, but he managed to round the foot of the bed and reach out for the chair to ease the weight off his leg. In doing so he miscalculated, his weight forcing the chair over backward. It careened into the second chair and both fell over with a muffled crash.

Guiltily then, Giff hobbled over to the chairs, straightened them and then stood listening, wondering if Mrs. Miles and Mike Keefer would be roused. He heard a movement in the kitchen, then hopped across to the bed, swung his legs up and pulled the covers over him.

On the heel of his movement the door opened and Kate stepped into the room, her dark eyes wide with apprehension. Her pale hair flowed softly down her shoulders and she hugged a gray wrapper about her.

"Was that you?" she asked.

Almost sheepishly Giff nodded. He was half-sitting up and she had surprised him in the act of reaching to turn down the lamp. Now he pushed himself to a sitting position.

"I slept for a while and couldn't go back to sleep. I thought I'd see if I could walk."

Kate came into the room frowning, then she sat down on the edge of the bed. "Did it work?"

Giff nodded. "I made it around the bed, then leaned on a chair. It gave way and I knocked them both over."

"You never quit, do you?" Kate observed.

"Now is no time to quit," Giff said brusquely. "Every hour I spend here means danger to you and your father, Mrs. Miles."

Kate said, dryness in her voice, "Don't you think you can drop the Mrs. Miles?"

Giff nodded, then said soberly, "Why don't *you?*"

Kate frowned and Giff continued, "There's no longer a Dan Miles." He paused. "Are you hoping the Mrs. will keep men away?"

Kate thought a moment and then said, "I've never thought about it that way, but maybe it's true."

"But all men aren't necessarily like your husband, Kate."

They both smiled at his first use of her name.

"Thank the Lord that's true."

"You're young, you're pretty, you're—"

"And a widow who made a bad choice," Kate interrupted.

"What's that got to do with anything?"

"If I was so featherbrained I would marry Dan Miles, maybe I would just pick another Dan Miles."

"You don't trust yourself not to?"

Kate's head dipped in acknowledgment.

"But how can you pick when you won't let yourself be chosen?"

"It's complicated," Kate said slowly. "I seem to see the seeds of Dan Miles in almost every man."

"Sam Furman?"

"Sam drinks too much. Dan did. Sam likes girls, the wrong kind. Dan did. Sam's in debt and always will be. Dan was."

Giff looked at her a long time, waiting for her to go on. He knew she was trying to put into words a feeling she didn't wholly understand herself.

"I feel sorry for you, Kate," Giff said finally.

Kate looked at him in surprise, puzzlement in her dark eyes.

"Your failure with him isn't something to hide behind," Giff said.

"Then what is it?" Kate asked bitterly.

"I always figured failure was nature's way of pointing to something better."

"Have you ever failed in something that important?" Kate's voice was soft and challenging.

"What do you think I'm doing now?" Giff countered.

"But you won't give up."

"No. Why should you, then?"

Kate had no answer. She rose, regarding him a long moment. He could not read in the stillness of her face what she was thinking. It seemed to him as if she were listening to some new and less troubling inner voice. Then she gave him the faintest of smiles, almost absent, turned and went out of the room, closing the door behind her.

Had he offended her? Giff wondered. As he reached up and turned down the lamp and slid deeper under the blankets he did not know whether he had or not.

Chapter Seven

TUCKER TIMED it so that he and Lee would arrive back at Dry Wells from their morning swing to the south while the stage was in. The rain had ceased during the night and the day was bright and clear. The smell of mud was everywhere and both their horses were plastered with it from chest to hoof. As they splashed up to the stage station, Tucker thought sourly how right Todd had been yesterday when he said the stolen herd could have been driven over the San Dimas range and never leave a track. The long rains had obliterated all signs and the circle they had made to the south this morning had turned up nothing.

The team change had already been hooked up and Kelsey's hostler was lounging against the muddy stage wheel, holding the reins for the coming of the driver. Tucker and Lee racked their horses and moved into the saloon. There was a murmur of voices from the restaurant but Tucker, spying the tall bearded stage driver,

Joe Mintern by name, at the bar, moved toward him,
Lee silently trailing him.

"Anybody turn up Ballew yet, Joe?" Tucker asked
and signaled to Kelsey for a bottle.

Mintern shook his head. "Corbett's quit looking in
town. He figured Ballew made it out of town."

Tucker felt the old rancor return. He downed his
whiskey and said, "He couldn't."

"Then he must be hiding in a full rain barrel,"
Mintern said. "They've looked everywhere else." He
pushed away from the bar and moved over to the dining
room. Halting at the door, he called, "Stage is ready."

Tucker poured himself another drink and pushed the
bottle toward Lee, who shook his head. Kelsey moved
over to collect the dollars from the stage passengers and
Tucker wanted to ask him if Hannah had left, but he
was too proud.

"You think he got away, Tuck?" Lee asked.

"Looks like it."

"Where would he go? If he was shot he had to get
help. He doesn't know anybody in this country."

"Anybody in the Breaks would hide him," Tucker
said sourly. "He's fighting us, isn't he?"

"He couldn't have made it to here. Nine hours in the
saddle on a wet night with a hole in him?"

Lee was right, Tucker thought. The sheriff hadn't
been sure where Ballew was hit but the buffaloed deputy
thought it was in the belly or the leg. A nine-hour ride
with either wound would have been impossible.

Then if he was out how did he get out? Tucker
wondered angrily. If he could have made it out of town
he might have flagged the stage, but the shooting had
happened after the stage had left. Could he have hidden
in a ranch wagon or freight wagon? That was unlikely.
Anybody discovering him would certainly have turned
him in for the reward or, if they'd been unable to
capture him, would have reported his location to Sheriff
Corbett.

Lee was right. Who did Ballew know in Harmony?
The hotel clerk for one. Oh yes, he'd put that advertise-

ment in the *Times*. Then he would know either Sam Furman or Kate Miles, or both.

Kate Miles. Tucker pondered this possibility and then he remembered the day he'd missed Ballew here by only minutes, Ballew had just finished a meal in the dining room. Hannah had said she'd fed him. Then Kate Miles had been eating with Ballew.

Now Tucker slowly straightened. Why would Kate Miles want to help Ballew? She and her father were so indebted to the Weybrights they wouldn't dare take Ballew's side. Besides, how could Kate Miles get him out of town?

Then it came to Tucker with a force of utter conviction. Kate drove a buggy from the Box K to work and back every day. She could have got Ballew out of town in that buggy.

A wild elation came to Tucker and he turned to Lee. "I know where Ballew is! Come on, let's ride!"

Lee asked, "Where?"

"Keefer's. Come on."

"Aren't we going to eat?"

"No time. Pick up a couple of cans of tomatoes and some crackers."

Lee straightened up. "Keefer's," he said, almost to himself. "You figure she'd hide him to get even with you for shooting Dan Miles?"

Tucker smiled grimly. "Hell yes. Why didn't I think of that before?"

Kate was no good to anyone including herself that morning. To begin with, Seth Parry had brought in an advertisement on behalf of the Weybrights stating the boundaries of the Circle W holdings and the names of the legal owners of the land; that all stock grazing on it was owned by them and that anyone trespassing on the property and taking or receiving Circle W stock would be prosecuted to the full extent of the law. Sam had jeeringly accepted the ad, asking Parry if it were necessary to restate what every rustler knew.

When Parry had gone, Kate had quarreled with Sam

over his treatment of Parry. She had argued this was no time to further anger the Weybrights. Giff was by no means out of danger and common sense dictated that she and Sam especially should be extra careful lest the Weybrights' suspicions turn on them.

"Parry knows I hate them," Sam had answered. "He'd be more suspicious if I were polite."

"It's not a beating you're risking, it's a man's life!" Kate had answered hotly.

"Oh, come now, Kate," Sam had scoffed. "My riding Parry is no threat to Giff. What's got into you?"

Because of their close association during working hours, Kate and Sam had an unspoken agreement that they would not eat together at the noon hour. Sam went to a boardinghouse and Kate to the hotel. During her dinner she reviewed their argument of this morning. Perhaps she had been unreasonable and she knew the reason why. It seemed to her that the most important thing in her life right now was to get Giff well and keep him hidden. She recalled Giff's words of last night and knew that Giff had been three-quarters right in what he had said of her. Instead of holding every man off at arm's length she should accept her failure with Dan Miles as simple bad luck. She wanted to marry and to have a family like any normal woman but it had taken Giff to point out how remote a possibility that was. What had he said? *How can you pick when you won't let yourself be chosen?* In his quiet way Giff had made her ashamed of her cowardice. *And it is cowardice,* she thought. Because she had given herself to one man and in effect been rejected, she had placed little value on herself and in her judgment. She knew she was afraid of being hurt again.

Men never came to court her now because she had rejected too many men before them. She had successfully pretended that Dan Miles had been the only love she ever had or would have. The roll of the sorrowing widow had only been a screen to hide her true feelings of self-doubt and disappointment.

Kate walked slowly back to the *Times* office in the noonday sunshine, and on the way made a sudden resolution that she would be different. To begin with, she would let it be known that any period of mourning she was supposed to be observing was ended. With no husband what was the sense of being known as Mrs. Miles? Why not Kate Keefer? Along with that change she could be warmer and more friendly to the men anxious to take her out.

In this mood of a new benevolence she entered the office, walked back into the shop and said abruptly to Sam, at the type case, "Sam, I was a fool this morning. I'm sorry I was so impossible."

Sam turned and looked at her, puzzlement in his face. "You apologizing?"

"I'm trying to."

"All right, you've apologized." He grinned. "You know, if we were married this would never have happened."

The old hostility rose in Kate and then she remembered her resolution. All the same Sam should be sidetracked. "How do you figure that, Sam?"

"If you were my wife you'd be home and looking after the kids."

"And living on what?" Kate said lightly.

"On money I wouldn't spend on booze and—other things."

"That's for some other girl, Sam."

Kate turned away and Sam laid an inkstained hand on her arm. "Katie, what is it?" he asked quietly. "I've been in love with you since the day you walked in and asked for a job. Is it that you can't get Dan Miles out of your head?"

"He's out of my head."

"And you'll marry some time?"

"I hope so."

"Anybody else ahead of me?" Sam asked slowly.

Kate's eyes widened in surprise. "Who would it be, Sam?"

Sam said simply, "Ballew." He watched her face.

Kate knew she was blushing and it angered her. "That's absurd!" she said hotly. "Why, I don't know the man at all."

Sam took his hand away and said quietly, "Think back, Katie. The day he came in here you were pretty rude to him. You were afraid he'd involve your father and reopen his quarrel with the Weybrights. Then he was hurt. You not only sneaked him out of town but you hid him and nursed him. What changed your mind?"

"Why, I'd take in a hurt dog!" Kate said angrily. "Where was he to go? Who was to take care of him?"

Sam shook his head. "From the way you talked, I would have thought you'd figure that was his business. Do you remember saying you wished he'd never come here and that you wished you'd never laid eyes on him?"

Kate was silent a long moment. "Then I have changed."

"That's what I'm saying," Sam said drily. "You come in here every morning all starry-eyed. You drop things, you forget things. Like this morning when you rode me about sassing Parry. You're like a mother hen with a new chick."

"Sam, that's not so!" Kate protested. "It's just that I've been living a humdrum life. All of a sudden there's someone to help and there's danger. Why would I be the same as I was a month ago?"

"I am," Sam said. He was silent for some time, watching Kate. She was frowning, considering what Sam had said. Was it possible that she appeared so changed to Sam? Wasn't he making it up, perhaps out of resentment for her fifteenth refusal to marry him?

"Then if it isn't Ballew, who is it?" Sam pressed.

"Oh, Sam, stop tormenting me!" Kate cried.

"Stop tormenting you?" Sam said wrathfully. "What the hell do you think you're doing to me every day?" He'd been holding a stick of type in his hand and now he slammed it down on the counter of the type case.

"I don't mean to," Kate said gently.

"You can't help it," Sam said, a kind of despair in his voice. "Finish up this piece and then lock up. I'm going out." He untied his apron, slipped it over his head, wadded it up in his hands and savagely threw it in the corner. He gave Kate a long, despairing look and tramped out.

Sam was headed for a saloon, Kate knew, and she felt pity for him. He was a good man, kind and generous to a fault. He would never turn out to be another Dan Miles, but that wasn't enough.

Now as she finished setting up the type that Sam had left, his words came back to her. In spite of her about-face in her relations with Giff Ballew, she saw nothing inconsistent in her actions. It was only common humanity and decency to help a man who was being hunted and hounded and hurt. If it had been Sam in Ballew's place she would have done for him exactly what she had done for Ballew, or for any other well-meaning but persecuted man. In fact, it was less a matter of helping an underdog than showing her hatred for a top dog.

Kate finished her work, locked up the shop and stepped out into the warm afternoon. She made two stops, one to pick up the copy for the hardware store advertisement, the other to buy some groceries before she went to pick up the horse and buggy at the livery.

She found herself looking forward to the return home with an eagerness that made her rein the mare in and examine her feelings. All right, she was eager to get home and to find out how Giff had progressed after a night's rest. Wasn't any nurse interested in the recovery of a patient? Also with half the afternoon off there were a lot of things around the house that should be tended to.

As she drove into the Box K, she saw Giff and her father sitting on the veranda. Giff was wearing clean clothes she had washed for him yesterday. She tied the mare to a ring set in one of the cottonwoods for Prudencio to unhitch later, took up her few parcels, waved to the two men on the veranda, and went in the kitchen door. Depositing her packages on the table she went into the living room off which Giff's bedroom opened and moved through the door onto the veranda. Her father motioned her to an empty rocker, saying, "Aren't you home early, Kate?"

"Sam's starting a drunk," Kate said, and now looked at Giff. He was freshly shaven and Kate saw almost with pain that his beard stubble had covered cheeks that were deeply gaunted. She looked for the cane. Giff noting her curiosity, said, "I'm through with Sam's cane, Kate. You can take it back to him in the morning."

"You made it out here by yourself?" Kate asked incredulously.

Giff nodded. "I've been cruising around the place without it."

Keefer rose now, saying, "I've loafed long enough. Giff's been telling me about those Wyoming winters. Me, I'll trade less grass for our open winters." He gave Kate's shoulder an affectionate pat as he moved past her, headed for the barn lot.

"What's Sam celebrating?" Giff asked curiously.

Kate felt her face flush as she said in a voice surprisingly controled, "He didn't say. Something bothers him now and then and he heads for a bottle."

"I hope you thanked him for what he did for me."

"I did, and he said, 'Tell him the only thanks I want is for him to get well.'"

They were silent a moment and then Kate said, "Giff, what do you plan?"

"Your father and I were talking about that," Giff said slowly. "I think the best thing is for me to hide out in the San Dimas. I'll meet up with fewer people who are after my hide."

Kate looked off at the barn lot and saw that her father was unharnessing her mare. "But after that?"

"Make as much trouble for the Weybrights as I can," Giff answered tonelessly.

Kate looked at him, and then beyond him. In the far distance she could see a pair of riders and now she rose. "Giff, it looks as if we've got company. You'd better get in your bedroom."

Giff rose and looked over his shoulder, saw two riders approaching, then moved easily toward the door into the living room. Kate followed him to the bedroom door and saw him lift his gunbelt from a chair and strap it on. As she went into the kitchen and started putting away supplies she'd bought in town, she felt her heart pounding. She could not imagine who the two riders were who were approaching, and ordinarily she would have assumed that they were coming to see her father on ranch business. Now, however, any visitor was to be feared.

She walked into the sparsely furnished living room, looking about to see if Giff had left anything lying about that would indicate his presence. There was nothing Kate could see that would give him away. He'd been hatless on the veranda which meant his hat was probably in his room. He had no other possessions except his gun and Sam's borrowed slicker which she had already returned.

Back in the kitchen, she put on an apron and started to make a pie crust for the apples which had been soaking on the stove since morning.

When, minutes later, she heard horses in the barn lot, she looked up, moving into the doorway. In that second Kate thought she would faint. Tucker and Lee Weybright, still mounted, were looking at her, and now both men touched their hats.

Pure terror held her motionless for a moment, and then she realized that it was too late to warn Giff. They had seen her. The only thing she could do was pretend mild surprise and welcome them.

Dusting her hands on her apron, she moved out the door and stood on the single step.

Tucker came through the gate, Lee trailing him. There was a look of excitement in Tucker's glance and wild dark face that chilled Kate's heart.

Looking beyond the Weybrights, Kate saw her father cutting across the barn lot toward them.

"Not working today, Kate?" Tucker asked idly.

"Sam's off on a drunk. He gave me the afternoon off." Kate's voice was surprisingly firm. "Looking for Dad? He's coming."

The Weybrights turned and waited until Mike Keefer came through the gate.

"Hello, Mike," Tucker said.

Kate noted with dismay that her father was not wearing a gun.

Keefer said affably, "Well, what brings you here, Tucker?"

Tucker Weybright said thinly, bluntly, "I think you're

hiding Giff Ballew." As he spoke he lifted out his gun.
"I'm going to have a look."

There was a long silence and Keefer's face was inscru-
table. Then he asked, "You got a search warrant?"

Tucker nodded. "And a badge." Without taking his
eyes from Keefer, he said, "Step out, Kate."

"I'll do nothing of the kind!" Kate said flatly. "What
do you mean bullying your way into a person's home?"

"I told you," Tucker said adamantly. "I think you've
got Giff Ballew here."

"He was shot, wasn't he? How could he get here?"
Kate demanded.

"I think you brought him in your buggy."

How did he know? Kate thought despairingly. Should
she turn and run in to warn Giff? No, the two of them
would surely shoot him down, and how could she or
her father keep him out of the house? She looked plead-
ingly at her father and Tucker intercepted her glance.

"Don't try it, Mike. I can shoot you and I will. I've
got the law on my side."

Kate glanced at Lee who was miserably embarrassed
and frightened. He would not look at her.

Tucker said then, "If you've not got him, what are
you worried about?"

"It's the principle of it!" Kate said shortly.

Keefer said, "Kate, go back in the house. Tucker and
I will talk this over."

"No, we won't!" Tucker said, and he shouldered
roughly past Kate and went into the kitchen.

She followed him, and Tucker halted and turned.
"Lee, come here!" he ordered.

Lee stepped into the room and Keefer followed him.

"Watch them both and keep them here," Tucker said
harshly. "There's bound to be a gun in this house."

Only then did Lee pull his gun and step in between
Tucker and Kate.

Tucker wheeled and moved into the living-room door
and halted, noting the big rug-covered sofa facing the
fireplace on his left and the doors on either side of the
big fireplace. He skirted the table behind the sofa and
headed for the door of Kate's bedroom.

Kate said to Lee, "I'm going in there. Shoot if you want to." She brushed past Lee who started to hold out a restraining arm. Kate pushed it away and Lee called, "Here she comes, Tuck," and let his arm drop. To Keefer he said, "Not you, though."

Kate came into the living room in time to see Tucker emerge from her room. He opened the next door which led to her father's room, looked behind the door and came out heading for the door in the near end of the room that led to Giff's room.

Hastily Kate said, "That's a locked storeroom, Tucker. I don't know where the key is."

"All right, I'll shoot off the lock," Tucker said. He was already in motion when the door opened and Giff stepped through. Giff said quietly, "I give up, Tucker." His gun was in its holster at his side.

"Oh no you don't!" Tucker said savagely, and his gun lifted. Kate screamed and now Giff, seeing Tucker's intent, grabbed the doorframe and pivoted back into the room as Tucker's gun went off with a bellowing roar in these confined quarters.

Then Kate, frozen with terror, saw Giff wheel back into the doorway, this time with his gun drawn. He shot swiftly.

Tucker's gun went off into the floor as he was jack-knifed inches into the air and beaten backward by the slug from Giff's gun which caught him in the chest. He made no sound except a whoosh of expelled breath before he fell heavily on his back.

Giff wheeled in time to see Lee and Keefer boil through the door into the living room. Lee's gun dangled from his hand, and then when he saw Tucker he halted so abruptly that Keefer crashed into him.

Lee took a step toward Tucker, then shifted his glance to Giff whose gun was held slackly at his side.

"If you're going to make your play, Lee, do it now."

Lee only shook his head and by that time Keefer was beside him. Keefer wrenched the gun from Lee's hand and the youth made no effort to retain it.

As if he were sleepwalking Lee slowly skirted the table, the deep armchair, and came to halt beside Tucker whose open eyes stared sightlessly at the ceiling. The dark and wild face shaped by violence was oddly peaceful now.

Kate sought refuge in her father's arms. She was shivering uncontrollably and Mike held her to him for the brief seconds it took her to control herself. Then she heard Giff's quiet voice. "I tried to surrender, Lee." Kate turned now to look at Lee.

"I heard you," Lee said quietly. The boy's face was white and held total shock.

Now Mike Keefer moved over to Tucker, knelt and felt for a pulse at his neck. Rising, he slowly took an Indian blanket that was on the leather sofa, shook it out, and covered Tucker's body.

Giff moved over to Kate, took her elbow and guided her out to the veranda.

"Sit down," Giff said gently.

Kate had started to shake again and she sank into a rocker, pressing her hands between her knees to stop the shaking.

"I didn't have a choice, Kate," Giff said.

"I know. I saw. He wanted to kill you," Kate whispered.

Now Lee and Keefer stepped out onto the veranda. Keefer still had Lee's gun in his hand.

Giff looked at Keefer and tilted his head, then stepped off the veranda heading toward the gate. Keefer followed him and when they were out of earshot of Lee, Giff halted.

"Well, Mike, it's happened just the way nobody wanted it to."

"It wasn't your fault. I heard it too, Giff."

"But you were hiding me," Giff said.

"Yes, I was, and I'm proud of it!" Keefer said angrily. The two men looked at each other and then Giff said, "Outside of calling in your loan, what's he apt to do to you, Mike?"

"I'm going to find that out right now," Keefer said flatly. "I'll go back with Lee and Tucker's body. I'll tell Lynch exactly what happened."

"And if Lee lies?"

'Kate will go with us." Keefer only then saw the dead weariness in Giff's face. "Why don't you go lie down? There's nothing you can do."

"Lie down!" Giff echoed blankly. "You think I'd stay here now?"

"You can't ride."

"I can if you'll give me a horse. I'm not going to pull any more trouble down on you and Kate, Mike." He paused and added bitterly, "The whole Circle W crew will be swarming over here when the word is out."

"Not if I can make Lynch see sense." He sighed and regarded Giff with a worried frown. "I'll give you a horse, Giff, but where'll you go?"

"I'll make out," Giff said quietly.

They both heard, at the same time, the sound of a man running and they turned to see Prudencio crossing the barn lot. He had doubtless been working away from the house and had heard the shots.

Now Keefer turned and called, "Lee, come here!"

Lee passed Kate, stepped off the veranda and came up to them. His handsome face was tear-stained and he made no attempt to hide the fact.

"You want Tucker's body taken to Circle W?"

"I—guess so," Lee answered.

"Then ride with us. I'll have a wagon hooked up," Keefer said.

Now Prudencio came through the gate and Keefer moved over to explain the shots and give him orders.

Giff shouldered past Lee, moved up to the veranda and halted before Kate. "I'll be going, Kate," he said quietly.

"But you can't!"

Giff said nothing.

"Where'll you go?"

"That'll work out. I just want to get out of here before I pull any more trouble down on you." He added grimly, "This is a fine way to thank you for all you and your father have done for me."

"It wasn't your fault," Kate said wearily, and now she stood up. "You'll need blankets and food. Let me get them."

She went into the house, managing to avoid looking at the figure under the Indian rug, and got two blankets from her father's room. In the kitchen, as she assembled cold meat and biscuits and a couple of cans of tomatoes, she thought that her world had suddenly come to an end. Giff would be off to be hunted again. She didn't know what punishment Lynch Weybright would mete out to her and her father, but it wouldn't be pleasant. They would probably lose this place and the work of five years. What was worse, though, was the prospect ahead for Giff. She didn't know if he could even ride.

Suddenly her hands paused as she began to understand the truth. *Why, I love him,* she thought. *Why did it take me this long to know it?*

Minutes later her father brought a saddle horse to the gate and Kate went out with the blankets and food which her father tied on Giff's saddle. Kate knew Giff was watching her, and she turned to him. "Will we see you again?"

"Yes," Giff said gently. "Keep remembering that. Yes."

Giff mounted with difficulty, shook hands with Mike, touched his hat to Kate, and rode off to the east.

When Giff was gone, Mike explained to Kate what they were going to do. There was no use waiting here for Lynch Weybright's wrath to strike them. They would both ride with Lee back to Circle W and explain Tucker's invasion and his attempt to kill Giff rather than capture him. Kate wearily agreed and went in the house to change into a blouse and divided skirt. While she was changing, Tucker's body was removed. Then soon afterward they set out for Circle W. Mike drove the spring wagon which held Tucker's tarp-wrapped body, and Lee and Kate flanked him as the cavalcade set out in the lowering dusk.

It was dark when they reached Circle W. Lee had gone ahead to break the news to Lynch, so that when the wagon drove in to the barn lot lanterns were lighted and the crew gathered around waiting for them.

As Kate reined in, she noticed that old Lynch seemed to have shrunk. In the lantern light his fierce eye seemed dull and only barely comprehending. In spite for her hatred for the old man and all he stood for, she could not help but feel pity. It was the saddest part of life, that a father should see his son dead before him, she thought.

"It'll be easier, Mike, if you drive the wagon up to the house. We'll put him there," Lynch said.

Her father nodded and clucked the team into motion. Kate followed the wagon while several of the hands carrying lanterns trailed along. Her father pulled up to the steps of the veranda. Kate put her horse ahead of the team, dismounted and tied the animal to the veranda rail. She watched in silence as four men, with others holding the lanterns high, took Tucker's body from the wagon, climbed the steps and went inside.

Mike Keefer swung off the seat and took Kate's hand. Together they climbed the steps and went inside.

They entered a high, long, combination living room and dining room. A lighted lamp was on the big dusty table. Directly across it Lee Weybright stood by an open door which led into a lamplit bedroom. There were two other doors in the same wall. The gallery extended above the doors and Kate saw that there were three rooms leading off it. She remembered then that when the Weybrights first came there had been Lynch and his two brothers with their families. As one of the brothers and then the other was killed in the fight for Circle W lands, their families had drifted off. What had been planned as the home for an empire-building family was now only a big, dusty, partially used house. The big dining table at the far end of the room was cluttered with gear that Kate could not distinguish in the darkness and off it the kitchen was unlighted and probably never used, Kate thought.

Now the Circle W hands with their lanterns trailed out of the room while Lee and Lynch remained inside the bedroom. Kate seated herself in one of the two big rawhide-covered chairs that flanked the cold fireplace at which her father stood, his back to its emptiness, teetering on his heels.

It was minutes before Lynch and Lee, both pale and

somber, returned to the big room. Lynch halted and looked at Mike, then at Kate.

"Why are you here, Kate?" Lynch demanded.

"To make sure Lee doesn't lie to you," Kate said.

"Let's see if you lie. Did you hide Ballew?" Lynch asked harshly.

"I did."

"How did you get him from town?"

"In my buggy."

"Why?"

"Because he was hurt and helpless," Kate answered.

Anger came into Lynch's face. "You know what this means for you and your father?"

Keefer said quietly, "Talk to me, Lynch. I gave consent. It means you'll call in my note."

Old Lynch nodded absently and then, clasping his hands behind his back, he moved slowly across the room, lost in thought. Then he turned and looked at Lee who was standing beside the other rawhide-covered chair. "What happened there, Lee?"

Lee cleared his throat and began on the story. Starting with Tucker's hunch as to Ballew's whereabouts, he told of their approach, their welcome, and of Tucker's abrupt demand to search the house. Tucker ordered him to hold the Keefers in the kitchen while he went through the bedrooms. Kate had refused to be held, Lee said, but he had succeeded in holding Keefer.

"The first words I heard," Lee said slowly, "were from Ballew. He said, 'I give up, Tucker.'" Then Lee paused and swallowed. "Then Tucker said, 'Oh no you don't,' and shot. There was an answering shot and then Tuck's second shot right on the heel of it. I ran into the room and there was Tucker lying on the floor, dying."

"How do you know Ballew didn't shoot first?" Lynch demanded angrily. "How do you know he didn't pretend to give up and then shoot Tuck?"

Kate cut in. "I saw it all. It happened the way Lee said."

Kate had been staring in defiance at Lynch, but now a movement behind him in the direction of the kitchen attracted her attention. The form of a man loomed in the dimness and was coming toward them. Kate wondered why Lynch would let one of his crew break in on this meeting, and then as the man moved closer down the long room and into the lamplight Kate saw with a shock of terror that it was Giff Ballew!

Her involuntary start made Lynch scowl, and then Ballew's voice came quietly into the room.

"That's the way it happened, Lynch."

Weybright wheeled and was looking into Giff's gun. Lee whirled too, startled, but he made no move to go for the gun in his holster.

Bafflement, hate, and anger were in Lynch's face as Giff slowly moved forward into the lamplight. Kate saw that Giff did not even look at her or her father, and with utter dismay she wondered how Giff could have been so insanely foolish as to come here now.

"Come to surrender, you killer?" Lynch asked harshly. Then he ordered, in the same hard voice, "Go turn out the crew, Lee!"

Now Giff halted in front of Lynch and he said quietly, "No, I didn't come to surrender. I came to make you a promise, Lynch." Lee did not move and Weybright said nothing. "I promise that the next time I see you or your son I'll try to kill you."

These cold implacable words brought a chill to Kate, and it was coupled with a feeling of revulsion and horror.

"You've done everything you could to kill me, including sending your son to murder me while I tried to surrender. I propose that treatment for you and Lee."

"You could start now," Lynch said bitingly.

"This is a warning only."

"I'll give you a warning of my own," Weybright countered. "I'll hunt you down and kill you if it takes forever."

Lee's voice came sharply now, "Dad!"

"Be quiet, Lee."

"I won't be quiet!" Lee shouted, and now he came over to confront his father. His face was white and his lips were trembling. "He means it and he'll do it, Dad! Can't you see that?" Lee said in a wild voice.

"Be quiet!" Lynch said sharply.

Lee said in slow wonder, "My God, what are you after, Dad? You've got two brothers dead and now Tucker. We'll all be dead. Can't you see that? *We'll all be dead!*"

"Not before he is," Lynch said in a granite voice.

"Oh, Dad, you're blind! Ballew has had a chance to kill me twice. He had a chance this afternoon and no one would have blamed him! He'll have a chance again!"

"Not if you're careful."

"Don't you see," Lee raged, "he has the chance now! I'm not going to live with that fear hanging over me. I'm going away. I want to get out of here!"

Lynch regarded him with open incredulity. "You're a coward," he said savagely.

But the torrent of Lee's words could not be dammed. "Sure I'm a coward, but I'm not a fool like you! You're fighting to save a ranch. Who're you going to give it to? Tucker? He's dead. Me? I'll be dead, or gone. You'll be left alone with a ranch that you've lied and cheated to get."

"Lee, go to bed!" Lynch said sharply.

"To bed, hell!" Lee shouted. "If I get out of here alive, my next bed will be in Montana. I've watched this too long. You destroyed that page from the deed book. You've set your crew on Ballew with orders to bring him in dead or alive. You've even posted a reward for him, so any drunk can kill him! You and Tucker have done every bad thing a man can do. Now Tucker is dead and you won't stop until I am!"

Lynch's face had gone ashen, Kate noticed. The young Lee that he had hoped to mold into another Tucker had turned on him and was about to desert him. Beyond that he had named him a cheat and a hirer of assassins and had blamed him for the death of his dearest son.

Lynch looked appealingly toward her father who was watching him with a grave hatred in his eyes.

Lee turned as if to go to his room, and Lynch said sharply, "Lee, wait! Where are you going?"

"Out of here—forever!"

"Wait!"

Lee halted and turned.

"What do you want me to do, Lee?" Lynch asked, his voice almost broken.

"Do?" Lee echoed, almost gently. He came back to face his father. "Do what any decent man would do. Call off your gunmen and your rewards. Give Ballew what belongs to him. It won't wreck us."

And now Lee looked at Ballew. "What do you want? Your original ranch back?"

Giff nodded. "And no more than that."

Lee turned to his father. "It's only a quarter of what we own, Dad! The cattle are ours. We can live with Aunt Myra while we build us a new house. What's more, we can live with a conscience—if we have any left!" He added almost gently, "Why are we fighting him?"

Lynch was silent a full minute but Lee would not go.

"Why?" Lee repeated.

Lynch finally asked with a kind of shyness, utterly alien to him, "If we did what you say, would you stay, son?"

"Stay!" There was almost incredulity in Lee's voice. "This is where I want to live, Dad, but I won't live the way we've been living."

Lynch's voice was oddly gentle, "Let's try it your way, Lee."

Lee took his father's arm and gently turned him toward the door. "If you mean it, the first thing you do is tell the crew that this manhunt is off."

Lynch looked over his shoulder at Giff and his eyes were unforgiving, Kate saw. Then he started for the door. Lee started with him, hesitated and came back to face Giff, who had holstered his gun. Lee put out his hand, and Giff accepted it. "I've wanted to do this a long time."

Then in sudden shyness Lee followed his father out of the room.

Giff moved across the room to Kate and halted before her.

"After I broke into the kitchen back there"—he tilted

his head toward the rear of the room—"and began to wait, I tried to remember what it was you asked me when I left your place."

"I asked if we'd be seeing you again," Kate said in a low voice.

That was it. Giff glanced at Keefer, then back to Kate, and a smile touched his gaunt face.

"You'll see me every day—if that's all right with you."

Cleive WCalhoun